THE GREAT FOX HEIST

JUSTYN EDWARDS

WALKER
BOOKS

First published 2023 by Walker Books Ltd
87 Vauxhall Walk, London SE11 5HJ

2 4 6 8 10 9 7 5 3 1

Text © 2023 Justyn Edwards
Illustrations © 2023 Flavia Sorrentino

The right of Justyn Edwards to be identified as author of
this work has been asserted in accordance with the
Copyright, Designs and Patents Act 1988

This book has been typeset in Stempel Schneidler

Printed and bound by CPI Group (UK) Ltd, Croydon CR0 4YY

British Library Cataloguing in Publication Data:
a catalogue record for this book is available from the British Library

ISBN 978-1-5295-0195-7

www.walker.co.uk

MIX
Paper | Supporting
responsible forestry
FSC® C171272

Praise for THE GREAT FOX ILLUSION

"A delightfully tricky tale of **magic** and **misdirection**. A **page-turner** that's also great fun to read."

M. G. LEONARD

"*The Great Fox Illusion* is a **glittering tale** of magic and mystery, trust and tricks, friendship and family. Let Justyn Edwards take you behind the scenes of a world of magic and illusion, on a **mind-bending adventure** to find the truth. Reading this brilliant book is like opening a **magician's box of tricks** and discovering their secrets for yourself."

THOMAS TAYLOR

"*The Great Fox Illusion* is **magic**! A page-turning mystery about family, friendship and magic tricks, told with real **panache** and **pizzazz**."

CHRISTOPHER EDGE

"This book did a **vanishing trick** on me – I didn't reappear until I'd read the very last page! A **spectacular, page-turning mystery** that will have you guessing until the ⬤⬤⬤ ies Justyn Edv⬤

very end, I can't wait to see what other stories ...

wards has up his (magician's) sleeve?'

CLARE POVEY

This book is a trick. Please don't trust it or sit back and enjoy it. In fact, don't take your eyes off it for a second, because by the end I'll have made a fortune in diamonds disappear from a vault, buried deep underground, surrounded by security guards and dozens of cameras, in one of the most secure banks in the world. A lot of very clever people will have tried to stop me and they will all have failed.

The question is, will you be able to work out how I did it?

Be assured that, like all tricks, there's a perfectly logical explanation. If you work out the method correctly, you're just the sort of person we're looking for. But if you decide to join our team, you'd better be prepared because things are getting very dangerous now. Events are spinning out of control, and no one knows where or how this will end.

PART ONE

Questions

In which the magician invites
you to take part in a trick.
But you're getting wise to this.
This time you will not be fooled.
You know that nothing
the magician says will be true.

1

The Vanishing Man

Magicians make you doubt. It's what they do for a living. While they're busy explaining how solid the box is, how it's nothing out of the ordinary, one of their hands is round the back opening a hidden compartment, doing the very thing they repeatedly tell you cannot be done. Deceit is in their nature; it is the very essence of who they are. This makes them somewhat difficult to trust.

Flick had come to the little Swiss town of Linth to find her father. That was what she wanted more than anything. It was what the Great Fox had promised. But when they arrived it turned out her father was nowhere to be seen, and the Fox had another reason for them being here. In other words, he had opened the hidden compartment.

In the TV trailer, Flick sat in front of the mirror while a make-up artist fussed over her, applying finishing touches to make her look presentable in front of the cameras. It was as if they were trying to cover over her disappointment, trying to hide her true feelings under layers of foundation.

The make-up girl stepped back to admire her work. "OK, that's you done."

Flick thanked her, stood up and then walked carefully out of the trailer, down the ramp and towards the backstage area. Here she was met by a very thin girl with pink hair, a nose ring and a headset. Her badge said *Gemma is happy to help*. Her scowl said otherwise.

Gemma urgently signalled to Flick. "Flick Lions is entering the stage area now," she barked into her headset. "Yes, I know she's late!"

"I've been in make-up," explained Flick as they were waved through a gate in the security fence by two burly guards.

"There isn't time," Gemma muttered into her headset. "She won't be because... You know. She's only got one..."

Tucking her hair behind her ears, Gemma looked at Flick, revealing a downturned mouth. No laughter lines. Always a bad sign.

"Actually," she said, "we're really pressed for time, so we're just going to film your bio here. Kevin will do you now."

Kevin turned out to be a forty-something pale-skinned man with a big tummy that was barely contained in his tight-fitting black overalls. He had a camera balanced on his shoulder and came down the steps from the back of the stage very slowly, as if worried his buttons might pop open.

Gemma turned to Flick. "Just hit Kevin with your name, age and something interesting about you, as if you were introducing yourself to the world."

At the bottom of the steps, Kevin spun round with a flourish and shoved the lens in Flick's face.

"Erm," Flick began.

Gemma rolled her eyes. "Name, age, something interesting. Let's go."

"My name is Flick Lions and I'm thirteen years old," Flick said as confidently as she could.

"Something *interesting*." Gemma snapped her fingers. "We'll try and stick it on afterwards. Like, do you love horse riding? Surfing?"

"I've never been horse riding," Flick said.

Kevin lowered his lens.

Gemma raised her eyebrows at him. "Did you get that?" To Flick she said, "That'll really get the viewers engaged. Flick Lions – never been horse riding. Compelling stuff."

She touched her headset and listened for a moment. "OK."

Kevin turned and gingerly made his way back up the stairs and Gemma gestured for Flick to follow.

Flick looked at the steps.

"Are we going to need—" Gemma started.

"I'll be just fine," said Flick, waving her away. She paused, took a firm grip on the rail with her right hand and started to move up the steps carefully, placing both feet on each one before attempting the next.

When she reached the top, she was met by a man with a headset who ushered her to stand in the wings, next to Charlie. Flick immediately felt herself relax a little when she saw him. He had on his familiar blue denim dungarees and a stripy top. Flick had never seen him wear anything else, although she was always pleased whenever she noticed the stripy top was a different colour, suggesting washing had occurred.

Charlie turned and beamed at her. "Hello," he whispered.

She smiled back. "Here we go again. How did we end up back here?"

"That's a good question," replied Charlie. "The Fox once said to me that a magic trick should be ninety per cent preparation and ten per cent performance. He's a great believer in planning any trick with multiple outs and having options ready if things go wrong, and sometimes even having whole backup tricks. I think the whole point of *The Great Fox Hunt* was to prepare for this competition. He knew this was coming. In fact, I would go so far as to say—"

"Shh," said the man in the headset.

"I think you're right," Flick whispered. "We should have seen this coming. If I had enough legs, I'd kick myself."

Charlie giggled. Then he lowered his glasses down his nose and looked at her over the top of them, pretending to disapprove.

Spotlights illuminated the stage and an elegant blonde stepped forward, wearing a dark business suit. Her perfect-for-TV glossy hair sparkled and a boom mic swung above her as she talked to the camera.

"Hello, my name is Christina Morgan, and it's my honour to welcome you to *The Battle of the Magicians*. Every ten years the Global Order of Magic holds an election to choose a new chancellor. But this time it's going to be different. Usually, the workings of the order are conducted in total secrecy, but this year they've agreed to let the cameras in, so you at home will get to see how the future of this ancient institution is decided. And believe me, this competition is all about the future. Each candidate will be represented by one or two young apprentices with great potential."

Christina spun round and gave her most dramatic look down the lens of a second camera: raised eyebrows, pursed lips, head slightly tilted. "So, let the battle begin!"

She gazed up into the lens of another camera above her. Bright graphics of fireworks shot across the giant screens at the back of the stage.

"Cut!" shouted someone from the wings.

Immediately three make-up artists rushed forward to tend to Christina's face as if it needed shoring up against erosion.

"And reset," came the same voice. "Go."

As quickly as they had arrived, the make-up artists scampered back into the wings and the graphics on the screens changed to a swirling blue mist.

Christina took a deep breath and furrowed her brow as if about to deliver incredibly tragic news. "There are four magicians standing for election," she said solemnly. "Their chosen apprentices will perform tricks and illusions, competing against one another over two rounds with two teams eliminated after the first round. To keep things scrupulously fair, the event will be televised so everyone at home will be able to witness the whole process."

She clapped her hands dramatically. "Right! We're now going to interview our first candidate standing for election. He's probably the most famous magician in the world right now, having recently come back from the dead – it's the Great Fox!"

The Fox walked on from the opposite side of the stage. He was wearing a black suit and white shirt and had on his trademark fox mask. He strode confidently towards Christina and stopped on his mark in front of her.

"So," said Christina. "Not content with faking your death and burning your own house down, you're now running for chancellor?"

"Yes," laughed the Fox. "It's been quite a busy year."

"It certainly has," she agreed. Turning to the camera, she added, "If you haven't seen *The Great Fox Hunt* yet, it's soon going to be available on catch-up." She beamed persuasively down the lens and then turned to face the Fox again. "Why do you want to be chancellor of the Global Order of Magic?"

"Because I think we're at an important turning point in history and the decisions we make now have never been more crucial."

"And you're mentoring the two apprentices you hired following *The Great Fox Hunt*?" asked Christina, clearly already knowing the answer.

Flick watched them from the wings. The Fox was never going to tell the truth. That it wasn't the future of the Global Order that mattered to him. He didn't care about its future or how it might become more relevant to a younger audience. What was important to the Fox was that whoever won the election also won the right to know the workings of any trick in the world. And that would include the method behind the Bell System – the greatest and most powerful trick ever created. A trick with such potential that some people would do anything to get their hands on it. The Fox had to win the election to keep it secret, and that meant Flick and Charlie had to win this competition for him, or at least that was what he had told them. But then again, he'd also said her dad would be in the Bahamas when Flick and her mum had flown there, and he wasn't. Apparently, he'd urgently needed to move on to hide the Bell System. And it was his wish that Flick help the Fox win this competition. Was any of it true? Eventually, Flick's mum had returned to the

UK because of her job, and she'd tried to persuade Flick to come with her. Flick had insisted on following the trail, doing all she could for her dad, but now there was a knot in her stomach because she was sure she was being played. She was on the verge of listening to her mum – just giving up and going home.

"Well, let's get them out here," exclaimed Christina. "Our old friends from *The Great Fox Hunt* – Flick and Charlie!"

Flick took a deep breath.

The screens lit up with red swirls as she and Charlie walked onto the stage and stood either side of the Great Fox. A camera spun round them, and the screens flashed with sparkles. The Fox struck a pose, standing side-on to the camera, while Flick and Charlie just tried not to look too awkward. When the director was satisfied, someone yelled "CUT!" and the screens went black.

The three make-up artists immediately returned to fuss around Christina's face, clearly worried what gravity might have done in the intervening three minutes. She held out her right hand and one of them placed her phone into it; she held out her left and a designer coffee was hastily given to her. She looked Flick up and down, grimaced, and then wordlessly walked off the stage. The make-up artists buzzed after her like flies.

Flick, Charlie and the Fox were directed off the stage, the Fox and Charlie both kindly pausing while Flick negotiated her way back down the steps. Their suitcases had been left here when they arrived, so Flick and Charlie collected them and walked through security, then out of the backstage enclosure, breathing a sigh of relief. The first ordeal was over. Now they could find their rooms.

They stepped into the bustle of Linth's harbour front. It was a beautiful summer afternoon, and the tourists were out in force, admiring the fishing boats and old bridges. The smells of cooking drifting from the street vendors made Flick's stomach rumble, but she didn't stop. From the harbour, she and Charlie followed the Fox into one of the side streets that turned steeply uphill, away from the waterfront. These cobbled streets were packed with people taking photos of the medieval clock towers and ancient shopfronts. Flick and Charlie pulled their suitcases along behind them and they rattled over the stones.

The Fox had been very quiet up to this point. Now he looked nervously over his shoulder and, when he was convinced no one was following them, said, "Don't trust Christina an inch. She doesn't want me winning this and I'm pretty sure she'll do everything she can to stop me. That means she'll come after you too."

"Don't worry. I'm not exactly one of her fans," muttered Flick.

"She's up to something – she keeps asking me questions about the Bell System. She shouldn't even be allowed to present a TV show after what happened last time, and yet here she is again. She definitely has some very powerful friends; maybe she's even still working with Drake. Everyone will do whatever it takes to get their hands on the Bell System. But we have one thing in our favour: this town is the backyard of my old friend Lukas De Haas – he owns the castle, and the local bank. We go way back, and he's a magician too. He'll look after you. You must keep an eye out for anything he might be able to throw your way during the competition and make sure you take advantage of it."

"And what about you?" asked Charlie. "You'll be helping us too?"

"The rules say I have to leave Linth after the opening ceremony when the competition officially begins tomorrow, and I'm only allowed back for the final trick. I can send you instructions every day, so I can still advise you, but other than that there is to be no contact between us. Have you got any questions?"

"Where's my dad?" asked Flick.

The Fox stopped walking. "I'm sorry. I was expecting him to be here to meet us."

"So where is he then?"

"I'm afraid I don't know."

"You promised me he would be here. Just like you promised me six months ago that I'd see him in the Bahamas."

"He promised me he would be here too. I don't know what's happened to him but I'm sure he's fine." He waved a hand dismissively. "I imagine he's just been held up somewhere, but I'll look for him."

The Fox resumed walking and Flick and Charlie fell in alongside him.

"Right now, we need to get to the hotel where all the apprentices will be staying. Lukas will meet us there. Don't worry about your dad."

Flick scowled but said nothing.

The street wound its way up the hill and near the top was the De Haas Hotel. Like most buildings in Linth, it was covered in ancient beams, murals and oriel windows – bay windows with fancy ornate woodwork. Flick looked up to take it all in. Atop the steep peaks of the old, red-tiled roof were a couple of Swiss flags fluttering in the gentle breeze. In case you'd forgotten where you were, she thought.

They weaved their way through the many tables and chairs in the square in front of the hotel. Here people were enjoying coffee, pastries and lunch while sitting under the collection of parasols that shielded them from the bright sun. Flick could hear people chatting in several languages, and nearby was a large stone fountain that gurgled away, providing the relaxing background sounds of running water.

The Fox led them to the old stone entrance. The doorway was so low that the Fox had to duck down to fit his masked head through. Flick and Charlie filed through behind him, blinking furiously as they stepped out of the bright light and into the cool, dark space of the foyer. They lined their suitcases up along a wall out of the way.

The Fox said, "I need you both to concentrate on the competition. Remember what's at stake here. Leave your father to me, Flick. I'll make sure he's absolutely fine."

And there it was. The man who lied for a living had made a promise. What could possibly go wrong?

While they waited for Lukas De Haas to appear, the Fox paced up and down and Flick glanced around the foyer. In one corner, tucked behind a curved wooden desk, was a girl with short brown hair. Very pale and frail-looking, she sat completely still. Maybe she needed to conserve energy, mused Flick. Even a man in a giant fox's mask doing laps of the foyer hadn't caused her to look up. Or perhaps this was normal in this particular part of Switzerland.

To the girl's right was a glass cabinet selling Linth key rings, postcards, calendars, pens, rubbers, mugs, fridge magnets, Post-it notes and china models of clock towers. The postcards looked faded and there was a layer of dust on the fridge magnets. Next to each item was an orange sticker with a large number on it. Possibly the price, or maybe how many years since the item was last purchased.

Gemma walked into the foyer and the Fox abandoned his pacing.

"Ah, here she is," he said. "Each team gets an assistant, and ours is the lovely Gemma."

Flick looked at Gemma. She had a laptop under her arm and a sense of irritation on her face. *Lovely* seemed a bit of a stretch. She was no longer wearing her *Happy to help* badge, which Flick took to be a bad sign.

Gemma met the Fox by the reception desk and opened her laptop.

"You need to see this," she said to the Fox.

Flick and Charlie crossed the foyer so they could see the screen, which was filled with a video showing a green door at the base of a tower.

"I was sorting out your flight paperwork when this popped into my inbox. Apparently, I need to show it to Flick and Charlie too." Gemma looked round to check they were watching. "Were you expecting Samuel Lions to join you?"

"Yes," said the Fox. "He was supposed to be meeting us here."

"Well, it seems he was … um. Better just watch."

The quality of the video wasn't good and there was no sound. It had been filmed in front of a stone wall with battlements along the top, in the middle of which was a large round tower. In the centre of this stood a green door. Flick guessed it had to be the De Haas castle that sat above the town. And in front of the door … stood a man in a large coat and a baseball cap. Next to him was a wooden cabinet about the size of a wardrobe and to the right, a little way along the castle wall, was a large red lorry with the Channel Seven logo on the cab door.

"That's your father," said the Fox, pointing to the man in the baseball cap.

Flick peered at the hazy figure. It might be her dad.

With the clothes he was wearing and the quality of the video, it was hard to tell. She watched with bated breath as her father opened the door of the wardrobe and got in. From behind the camera half a dozen people, clearly film crew as they were all wearing black overalls, advanced towards the wardrobe. Flick couldn't work out what they were carrying at first, and then she realized they each held a power tool.

The crew went to work. They removed the door and the sides until there was nothing left of the wardrobe. Her dad had vanished. The crew placed the parts in a pile in front of the lorry. One poured liquid all over the pile before dropping a match. The flames shot up so brightly the camera struggled, and the colours distorted.

Another crew member climbed up into the cab of the lorry. There was a pause, and then the lorry inched slowly forward, driving right over the burning pile. Next it reversed back over it. Then it moved forward and, once again, drove over the flattened, charred remains.

At that point, the film ended.

"Apparently your father told the crew this trick was supposed to be part of the TV show," Gemma said. "But it wasn't. It was never scheduled to be filmed. No one knows why he did it and no one knows where he is now."

"What do you mean?" cried Flick.

"Well, as far as the crew's concerned, he climbed into that wardrobe and vanished into thin air."

2
The Voice

Gemma had left as she was needed to help build the stage up at the castle. The Fox had gone back to his pacing. Charlie was biting his lip anxiously. Flick just felt sick.

She bombarded the Fox with questions. "Why would he do that? Why would my dad disappear like that?"

But the Fox didn't respond. He didn't even seem to notice her. He just walked round and round the foyer with his head bowed.

Eventually he stopped and muttered, "I've got to go. You two stay; Lukas will be here any minute."

And with that, he walked out.

Flick and Charlie stood helplessly in the foyer and wondered what to do.

"Do you think the Fox even cares about my dad?" Flick asked. "They're supposed to be friends! Or is he just worried about himself?"

"To be fair," said Charlie, "I think he's thinking about a lot of things at once. He seemed to have the weight of the world on his shoulders a few weeks after we arrived in the Bahamas. At first, he was really excited about the training we were doing, especially how good you were getting at using the Fox Files, but then he became distracted. I think he probably does care – he's just not very good at showing it. Although I can see why you might think he's not interested, as he's very bad at showing empathy. Some of that might be down to the fact that you can never see his face under that fox mask, but I suspect a lot of it is just down to the stress he's under…"

Flick let Charlie ramble on, but said nothing. She was unconvinced.

When Charlie finished his monologue he lapsed into silence, and they both stood thinking about what had happened and what it might mean. As they waited, a couple of tourists came into the hotel and approached the desk. The pale girl finally looked up. Would they place an extensive key ring order? Sadly, the tourists just walked past the reception desk and up the stairs.

"Ah, there you are," called a voice.

A tall man in black silk trousers and matching waistcoat stooped as he passed through the tiny entrance door. He had long dark hair tied back in a ponytail, a goatee beard and a large hooped earring in his left ear. The cuffs on his white dress shirt were undone, as were the top few buttons, revealing several gold necklaces. He looked like a very rich pirate. If Rolls-Royce made seafaring men, thought Flick, they would come off the production line dressed like this. Following him was a large Doberman. It strolled in through the door obediently at his heels.

"I'm Lukas De Haas, and I must say it's a massive pleasure to finally meet you two. The Fox has told me a lot about you." The man reached out and vigorously shook both their hands. Charlie coughed. The smell of his aftershave was almost overpowering.

Lukas looked around. "Where's Foxy?"

"He's gone. You've just missed him," said Charlie apologetically.

Lukas glanced down at the dog. "Stay," he commanded. The dog parked his bottom just inside the doorway and regarded Flick with a cold stare.

"What's your dog called?" Charlie asked.

"This is Nero," said De Haas.

Flick moved to stroke him, but Lukas laughed. "I wouldn't. He's not had his lunch yet. Anyway, never mind about him. Let's get you checked in."

He strode over to the pale girl at the desk. Maybe she'd been conserving all her energy for this moment, because she actually smiled and stood up. This was the hotel owner after all. Burning valuable calories, she even managed to walk to the wall behind her desk and return with swipe-card keys for Flick and Charlie, which she handed to De Haas. Then she plonked herself back on her chair, exhausted.

Lukas gave them each a key card. Flick took hers and noted that it was white with a large orange fox's head on it.

"You'll need these to access the rooms upstairs," he said. "When you get to the top of the stairs, turn right, and your rooms are straight on down the corridor. But first you need to watch an induction video in there." He gestured to an open door opposite the reception desk. "You can leave your bags here, and then when you've watched it you are definitely going to want to see what's out in the car park. We've built an HQ for each team. This will be your base for the duration of the competition. Those keys will also get you into there."

"Oooh," said Charlie excitedly. "How do we get to the car park? Is it down there?"

"Down that corridor past the stairs." Lukas pointed. "You can't miss it. Induction video first!" he called as Flick and Charlie scarpered in the direction of the car park.

Flick and Charlie reluctantly retraced their steps. The induction room was a small space containing a large TV on a stand with a green leather sofa in front of it. There was a message on the screen which said: *Welcome, Felicity and Charlie*. Under this it said: *Press to play*. Charlie walked to the screen, tapped the play icon and the two of them sat down on the sofa.

A woman appeared on the screen standing in front of a plain white background. She had shoulder-length grey hair and wore a purple cape that was fastened with a silver brooch.

"My name is Ursula," she said smoothly. "I'm the current chancellor of the Global Order of Magic. Welcome to this competition to appoint my successor. Every ten years we hold an election to decide the new chancellor, but this year is different. We want to connect more with a younger audience, hence the cameras, and this is of course why each magician standing for election has chosen to be represented by either one or two apprentices. These young magicians will compete to win the election for their mentor, and to keep things fair I will be the judge.

"Outside in the car park you will find the headquarters of Team Fox. Each base has been themed to make you feel at home, and yours has been designed to look like the library at the Fox's Den. You'll see we've given you both the gifts you requested to help you settle in."

At this, Ursula paused as if waiting for her generosity to be acknowledged.

"Flick, you have been gifted a Fox pod. You can use this to gain access to the Fox Files, the digital library that the Great Fox has compiled of every trick ever performed. If film footage of a magician exists, you'll find it here, along with biographical information, schematics and diagrams of their creations, and also plenty of 3D performances. The Fox pod comes with a set of virtual reality goggles and gloves so you can interact with what you see, and you'll find the floor moves when you're sitting in it, so you can move your feet to walk around the VR environment."

Flick didn't need to be told about the pod. She had spent hours in one of these over the last six months.

"There was some debate about whether you should be allowed to have this," admitted Ursula. "But some of the other contestants have also requested and received gifts that will help them, so we didn't feel it would afford you an unfair advantage.

"And, Charlie," she continued, "you have been gifted what you asked for: a freezer full of ice cream. Enjoy! I'd like to wish you both all the best in the competition, and I look forward to seeing how well you do."

The video ended and the screen went black.

"Oooh, yes!" exclaimed Charlie, leaping up. "Let's go and take a look at our base!"

Flick stood up more slowly and followed him. They crossed back through the foyer and made their way down the corridor to the right of the stairs. The red carpet continued here, but the walls were painted plain white.

"So," Flick said slowly, "I asked for a Fox pod, which will actually help us win the competition, and you asked for ice cream?"

"Hey!" Charlie protested. "Ice cream helps me think!"

The corridor ended in glass double doors, giving Flick and Charlie a clear view of the HQs. Eagerly they pushed through the doors into the car park, taking in the large structures standing in a line like four wooden forts. Each one had a ramp leading up to a large glass sliding front door with windows either side, and a flat roof with a flag flying above.

The second fort from the right had a large fox's head engraved on the door and printed on the flag. The symbol matched the one on their key card. The fort to the right of theirs had a lightning bolt, and the other two were decorated with a three of clubs symbol and a silver cane.

"The three of clubs is the sign for the Studio Three Crew," said Charlie.

"And the lightning bolt," Flick said, "has to be for Synergy."

"The silver cane can only be for Dominic Drake," muttered Charlie. "So pleased he's here."

They walked up the ramp to their fort and Charlie swiped his card on a reader by the door. It swished open and they entered.

Inside, they could see that Ursula's description was spot-on. They were most definitely in a library, with books from floor to ceiling. There was an old wooden table and chairs with a chandelier hanging above, and even a fire on one wall with a couple of armchairs in front of it. On a second look, Flick could see the fire was actually a TV screen showing some flickering flames. At the back of the room, on the left-hand side, was the Fox pod, and there was a freezer behind the table and chairs on the right. On the back wall was a large orange fox's head.

Charlie went straight to the freezer and opened it.

"Oh, they've given us a great mix here."

"Us? So I'm allowed some, am I?"

"Of course. What a selection! There's honeycomb, and chocolate mint, and coconut, and mango, and banana, and strawberry..."

Flick froze. She could hear another noise. What was it? It sounded like someone breathing.

"...and Oreo—"

"Shh!" she whispered.

"What?" asked Charlie, frowning.

"Shut up a minute."

Flick listened hard as she slowly spun round. The room was empty. But there was definitely the sound of breathing. It was unmistakable.

Hello, Flick.

Charlie jumped.

The voice was so deep it resonated inside Flick like a thousand claps of thunder. It seemed to come from everywhere at once and nowhere at all. It was as if the wind was talking.

Where is the Bell System?

Flick frantically scanned the room, trying to work out where it might be coming from.

You will tell me.

Flick pressed her back to the door and Charlie stood stock still by the freezer. There was nothing on the ceiling or walls. No sign of any speakers or electronic boxes that could be the source.

Do you want to know what's happened to your father?

"Where is he?" asked Flick, swallowing hard.

I see that got your attention.

"What have you done with him?"

The voice gave a soft chuckle.

If you want to see him again, you'll tell me where the Bell System is.

"I don't *know* where it is."

Don't lie to me, Flick. I see everything. I'm everywhere. When you leave this room, I'll be with you. When you take part in the competition, I'll be watching you. Everything you do, I can see.

"I really don't know where it is!" she cried. "I think … I think my dad might have it or has hidden it somewhere, but I don't know where."

I want you to ask the Fox where it is. Get him to tell you.

Flick stood in silence.

If you want to see your father again, you'll do as I ask.

"OK. I'll ask him. But how will I let you know what he says?"

There was that chuckle again.

Don't worry about that. I will know.

"Just don't do anything to my dad, OK?"

I will keep my word. Unlike the Fox. You know he's lying to you, don't you?

Flick was silent.

Oh, I see that you do know. You're not sure if you should trust him. Well, let me speed things along for you. The Fox is after a painting. And when he explains that, you'll know what he really wants.

"What do you mean?"

You'll see. All he really cares about is getting the painting. It's the reason we are all here.

"What painting?"

Flick waited for a response but there was silence. The breathing had stopped.

"Hello?" she called.

Nothing.

"Are you still there?" she asked.

But there was only silence.

3

The Bank

Flick was shaking so much she had to sit down in one of the armchairs. Charlie slowly walked over and joined her.

"What on earth was that?" he exclaimed.

"I have no idea."

"Where was the voice even coming from?"

"It felt like it was in my head. But you could hear it too?" she asked anxiously.

"Yeah, it sounded as if it was coming from everywhere."

"My dad is in danger. I think he was trying to send me a message with that trick before – and now there's this. We need to find him, Charlie."

Charlie looked awkward for a second. "But ... I mean, doesn't it seem like he might not want to be found?"

"He needs my help!"

"I don't think he sees it like that. He's trying to protect you. If he wanted to see you, he could try and find you somehow. But he seems to be trying to do the opposite, to hide from you, maybe even get as far away from you as possible."

Flick shook her head.

"I think you need to respect that he might not want help. In fact—"

"If it was your family, wouldn't you do anything to help them?"

Charlie opened his mouth to say something and then thought better of it. He nodded.

"Exactly," said Flick. "Anyway, we'd better go. We've still got to take our cases up to our rooms."

They stood up and Charlie swiped his card, so the door reopened. They walked back down the ramp, through the glass doors at the rear of the hotel and down the corridor towards the foyer. Here they found the Fox had returned and was pacing up and down impatiently while Lukas was leaning against the reception desk looking a bit bored.

Seeing them, the Fox said, "Come on. We're expected at the bank. They're waiting to do some introductory filming for your big trick and we don't want to be late."

"We haven't even come up with our first-round trick yet," said Flick, "so why are we starting with the second round?"

The Fox looked at her. She could see his eyes glinting

through the holes in his mask as he said, "The trick you will perform for the second round is nothing short of a masterpiece. It will require total dedication and practice from day one to be ready to perform it."

"But we haven't taken our bags up to our rooms yet," said Charlie.

"Well, get a move on then," said the Fox, shaking his head.

Carrying their key cards and suitcases, Flick and Charlie headed up the grand staircase. It had wooden banisters and a plush red carpet, and Flick was relieved that the steps were wide and the gradient was shallow. In fact, they were the easiest steps she had attempted in a while. At the top, they turned right onto a landing where the walls were covered in cuckoo clocks and old photos. Flick paused to look at them. Apparently, they used to make the clocks in this building. Although, judging by the number still hanging on the walls, she thought, they hadn't sold many. As they passed down the landing, they saw rows and rows of them in different sizes, colours and shapes.

"Hopefully none of these are working," said Charlie as he regarded them sceptically, "or else sleeping in this hotel will be impossible."

Flick and Charlie had adjacent rooms. Flick inserted her key and the door swung open. Her room was small and neat and had all the features one would expect. Television, en suite with a shower and a bath, telephone for room service, a desk with a chair, wardrobe, lamps. Mock Alpine chalet-style eighteenth-century wooden clock with two-tone cuckoo. The usual.

Flick closed the door and quickly unpacked. Unzipping her suitcase, she hung her clothes in the wardrobe and put her toiletries in the bathroom. It all seemed nice enough, but she couldn't enjoy any of this. Her brain was still racing. How could she find her dad?

She reached into her pocket and took out her phone. The Fox had said she would need to hand it in at the start of the competition after the opening ceremony, so she had time for one last quick chat with her mum. She scrolled through her contacts and put the phone to her ear.

"Hi, Mum."

"Flick! Have you got there OK?"

"Yep, arrived safely."

"What's the hotel like? Is it really old and full of cobwebs?"

Flick smiled. "No cobwebs, but lots of cuckoo clocks."

"Cuckoo clocks?"

"You know, the famous clock made in Switzerland. When it chimes a little bird pops out of the front and makes a cuckoo noise."

"Oh."

"Exactly."

"Why?"

"That's a good question," said Flick. "All I know is they're very proud of them here."

"And does the bird mind?"

"It's not a real bird!"

"Oh. Anyway," continued Flick's mum, "did you finish your maths homework before you left?"

Flick rolled her eyes. "Yes, I told you I'd done it. All finished."

"Good. It was very kind of the Fox to arrange a tutor for you while you were in the Bahamas. Your education is very important. The Fox is good to you."

"Is he? It was good of the Fox to pay for a tutor for me and Charlie, but Dad isn't here. And I think the Fox is more concerned with furthering his own career than finding him."

"He's not there? Aargh! This is typical of your father. You know my feelings on this. It is what I said to you when I left the Bahamas – I don't mind you having fun with the magic but don't try and find your father. You cannot live your life for him. I certainly won't."

"I just saw a film of…"

"Of what?"

"It doesn't matter."

"I suppose he might turn up eventually. In the meantime, stay with the Fox. People are complicated, Flick. Be patient."

"Well, that is definitely true. Anyway, I'd better go; the others are waiting for me. We're allowed to video call every day, so we'll talk soon."

"OK. I am sorry about your father. Try and have fun, *meu amorzinho!*"

Flick smiled and hung up. She was putting her suitcase away in the bottom of the wardrobe when there was a knock on the door.

"Ready?" called Charlie from the corridor.

Flick opened the door. Charlie was examining one of the clocks on the wall opposite her room.

"Why cuckoos?" he asked.

Flick shrugged.

"Why not a different bird or animal? Why are cuckoos so desperate to tell us the time? Now, a cockerel clock would make sense, although that would only be interested in telling everyone the time in the mornings…"

Flick tuned Charlie out as they made their way along the corridor. She thought about what her mum had said. Should she just do what the Fox told her?

"Who decided it should be a cuckoo?" Charlie continued. "And what did they base that decision on? Is there any evidence that they're particularly punctual birds?"

Flick decided that at the moment she didn't really have much choice.

When they reached the top of the stairs Charlie slowed so he could walk beside Flick, and they descended at a comfortable pace. Back in the foyer, Flick nodded to the pale girl behind the desk, but she clearly didn't have the energy to respond. There was no sign of the Fox or De Haas, but Nero was still sat near the entrance. He regarded Flick with dark eyes.

They gingerly stepped past him and ducked out of the low stone doorway into the square. De Haas and the Fox were waiting for them.

"Let's go," ordered the Fox.

They passed the tables occupied with families snacking and enjoying their coffee, and the fountain bubbling happily away in the afternoon sunshine. Flick walked beside the Fox as they plodded up the hill.

He seemed to hesitate before speaking. "I know you're upset about your dad disappearing, but I need you to concentrate. The way to get your dad back is to win the competition and keep the workings of the Bell System safe."

"Where *is* the Bell System?" Flick asked.

"Your dad is with it, and the best way to help him come home is to win the competition."

Flick nodded stiffly. She refused to give the Fox anything more. Sure – the best thing was to help him become chancellor of the Global Order. Of course it was.

"Once I'm chancellor we won't need to worry about anyone else getting access to the Bell System. And your dad is going to make sure it's hidden such that no one will ever be able to find it."

"Do you know that for sure?"

"He's not exactly filled me in on all the details of his plans," the Fox continued. "Now!" He clapped his hands. "To win this competition we need to perform an amazing trick.

Competing against us are Synergy and the Studio Three Crew, not to mention Dominic Drake, who has chosen Harry and Ruby as his apprentices. So, the trick we perform has to be brilliant to stand a chance. And that means the preparation starts now."

They continued uphill through the throngs of tourists. Flick couldn't believe she was competing against Harry and Ruby again. Last time they had met they were secretly working with Synergy, but it looked like that partnership was now over – unsurprising given how things had ended. Flick hadn't exactly hit it off with either of them and given what had happened at the end of *The Great Fox Hunt* they must hate her now.

Eventually, they came to a large square where another stage had been constructed. There was an area in front of it cordoned off for the audience and plenty of crew bustled about setting up lighting and sound kit. A red lorry with a Channel Seven logo on it was round the back of the stage being unloaded. On the stage was the tall skinny guy from Synergy; Flick recognized him instantly – he had very long arms and legs and looked spindly and delicate. He'd dyed one side of his Afro blond and appeared to be wearing a metallic blue shell suit. With him was a boy in a similarly hideous outfit. They looked like they were practising some sort of trick with a couple of large metal hoops. The Fox turned to look at them but didn't comment, or slow down. They kept hustling up the hill.

Above them, Flick could see the walls of the castle. She studied the outline of the ramparts and the tower, sure that was where her dad had performed his disappearing trick. She felt a pang as she thought of him hiding in a cabinet that was then dismantled, set on fire, and then run over. Why on earth had he done that – and where had he gone? The email to Gemma had said she was to be shown the video. What was her dad trying to tell her?

And then, striding down the hill towards them, she saw Dominic Drake with Harry and Ruby. Drake was leading the way, twirling his cane self-importantly. Despite the summer sunshine, he was still in his black suit with a green handkerchief artfully poking out of the breast pocket. Harry followed dutifully behind him and Ruby was at the back. Harry looked at Flick and then turned away impassively, but Ruby gave her a little wave. Flick was just waving back when Drake spotted her. He shook his head at her in contempt and then looked ahead, not breaking his stride.

The Fox slowed so that Lukas could come alongside him and then he murmured, "I want you to keep an eye on Drake and his apprentices. They're dangerous."

"Oh, don't worry, I will be," Lukas replied. "This is my town; I know everything that goes on here. There isn't an inch of it that isn't covered by cameras. There's one on every lamp post. They won't be able to sneeze without me knowing about it."

"Good," said the Fox. "Make sure you let me know what they're planning. They're probably our biggest threat, and we can't afford to lose."

Lukas chuckled. "Well, what you're planning at the bank is definitely impressive."

What was that? Flick bumped along behind them, only half concentrating. The more she thought about it, the more her suspicions increased. Everyone seemed to be in agreement that the most important thing in the world was helping the Great Fox become chancellor of the Global Order of Magic. No one was interested in finding her dad. The Fox had distracted them all, but she was determined she would not be fooled.

4

The Wager

The bank had an impressive old facade with long sash windows and a steep sloping tiled roof with high V-shaped gables in the style that the Swiss seemed particularly to enjoy. But they didn't enter the building. Instead, the Fox led them into a bakery opposite. They walked past some tasty-looking cakes on display in the window and stepped into the crowded little shopfront which smelt of freshly made bread. They passed the counter and ducked through into a back room, where the TV crew were waiting for them.

The Fox and De Haas started to discuss with a bald man where the cameras were going to be set up while Flick and Charlie waited patiently in the doorway.

Gemma appeared brandishing a very official-looking clipboard. "We're going to film you on the roof meeting De Haas, who owns the bank opposite. You will not speak in the interview. Your job is solely to be introduced to Mr De Haas and shake his hand. There are stairs so we need you to get a move on. Understood?"

"Lovely to see you too," said Flick.

Gemma gave Flick a hard stare. "Time is money, Miss Lions. But, OK, since you want to chit-chat, do you like the look of the bank you're going to rob?"

"What?" Flick's mouth dropped open. "Rob what now?"

"Didn't he tell you?" Gemma smirked, but she didn't wait for an answer. She had already moved on to talk to the bald man. Such a big clipboard, so little time.

Flick headed wide-eyed to the bottom of the stairs and set about climbing them as fast as she could. It took her a while as they were narrow, steep and twisty. What on earth was the Fox really planning to do in the bank, and when was he planning on letting them know?

As she reached the top, the Fox, Gemma and Charlie came up behind her and they all stepped onto the roof. Here there was a large flat section overlooking the bank with views across Linth. It looked stunning in the sunshine.

"Wow," marvelled Charlie. "I can see why this would make a dramatic location for filming."

Lukas De Haas and the TV crew joined them, and Gemma

ordered Flick and Charlie to stand behind the Fox – Flick on his left and Charlie on his right. They faced a grinning De Haas, his long mane of hair blowing rakishly in the wind. His cheeks were aglow, making him look like he'd been at the rum.

The camera was on a boom, and it took in the view across Linth before swooping towards the Fox. As it panned in, he started to speak.

"This is Lukas De Haas, owner of the magnificent bank we can see behind us. Mr De Haas, thank you for joining us. Tell us a little about your bank."

Lukas nodded. "My family has owned it for more than three hundred years. During that time, we have offered private banking and wealth management services to Europe's elite."

"And is there a vault in the bank?" asked the Fox.

"There is. It is deep underground, and has a steel-reinforced concrete door over a metre thick operated with a dual-action combination lock. No one has ever breached our security."

"What is the most valuable item in your vault?"

"There are some diamonds that belong to my family. They are worth around twenty-five million euros."

"Mr De Haas, are you a betting man?"

"I enjoy an occasional flutter."

The Fox paused while he waited for the camera to zoom in even closer. "In that case, I'm going to make you a wager. I bet that these two children can make those diamonds vanish."

The camera zoomed in on Flick and Charlie, who hastily tried to look solemn rather than nervous.

The Fox continued. "These kids are about as far from experienced bank robbers as you can get, but I'm telling you that they will remove those diamonds from the vault without setting off any of your bank's security measures or damaging the vault itself. I can also tell you that the theft will take place at exactly 9.30 p.m. this Friday, and it will all be captured on film."

Flick miraculously kept her face impassive for the camera.

Lukas laughed loudly. "That is a fantasy, I'm afraid. We have an exceptional security team."

"I'm sure you do."

"No one has achieved what you are suggesting in three hundred years. And believe me, plenty have tried."

The Fox stepped forward across the roof and offered his hand, which De Haas shook.

"It seems we have a deal, Mr De Haas. Flick and Charlie will do what has never been done before. They will do the impossible."

5

The Vault

Flick and Charlie walked through the large double entrance doors of the bank into an elegant and welcoming space of white polished marble. Facing the entrance were a row of cashier stations behind a marble desk topped with glass. The ideal location to film the Great Fox directing one of his most impressive tricks yet.

Lukas De Haas led the way across the grand foyer, followed by the Fox and the camera crew, and then Charlie and Flick. One of the cashiers behind the desk smiled and waved as they approached a side door. Flick frowned. The bank staff wouldn't be so welcoming once they realized their guests were there to plan a heist, she thought. The door had an electronic lock and Lukas dug out a card from his waistcoat pocket to open it. They passed into a short corridor, at the end of which was a second locked door. On the other side were some staff toilets and another passageway. Halfway down was a serious-looking metal door. De Haas swiped his card again, and everyone filed through.

The room they now found themselves in was less than four metres square. With Lukas, the Fox, Charlie, Flick, a camerawoman *and* a man with a boom microphone inside, it was quite a squeeze. Flick breathed in and wedged herself into a corner.

"This is the bank security control room," De Haas said imperiously.

Sitting with their backs to them were three white-shirted guards watching an array of TV monitors. There were four large screens in front of each of them, all cycling through live feeds from different CCTV cameras.

"Three guards constantly monitor CCTV cameras placed all over the building. Twenty-four hours a day, seven days a week."

Flick watched the images cycle across the screens. Some showed the street outside while the rest looked to be inside the bank. There were several of the foyer from different angles.

"The only access to the vault is via a lift and the only way you can activate that lift is from here. An eight-digit pin needs to be entered into the master computer for the lift to descend. This number is changed daily."

De Haas said something to the guards in German and they laughed as he opened the door again and Flick could finally escape the cramped space. They all tumbled out. Lukas led the way further down the corridor to the lift. He picked up a telephone next to it and asked for the pin to be entered in the control room.

After a few seconds, the lift doors opened.

"Danke," he said into the phone.

The lift was surprisingly large and all six of them fitted in with room to spare. It only had two buttons: G and B. Lukas pressed B, and the doors closed. They descended smoothly to the basement and the doors opened onto a plain concrete service corridor.

"Access to the vault is down this corridor," Lukas informed them. "It is monitored by two CCTV cameras, one at each end."

They all dutifully looked at each of the cameras as he pointed to them. Flick resisted the urge to wave. They walked down the corridor until they came to a large round door on the left wall.

The vault.

"The vault is a steel-reinforced concrete box, more than a metre thick. The good news for you is that there is no CCTV in there. But this is because the vault is completely sealed – so no access for wires. This is the only reason why we are allowing you to put a camera in there."

"My viewers need to be able to see the magic happen," explained the Fox.

"It won't be able to transmit live, you realize? Too much steel and concrete."

"Yes. That's fine. It's a stand-alone unit. It will record to disk."

Lukas nodded. "You do know that if the alarm goes off, your camera will be removed by security? Everything – and everyone – will be ejected immediately from the bank."

"I understand."

"My insurers insist on it. If the alarm is triggered, then all foreign objects will be removed from the building. That will include you."

The Fox laughed. "I'd better make sure Flick and Charlie do a good job then, hadn't I?"

A thought suddenly occurred to Flick. Maybe there was a way to pay the Fox back for all his secrets. What if she triggered the alarm deliberately and got them thrown out of the bank?

They all stood and looked at the vault door. It really was impressive, for a door.

De Haas continued with his lecture. "The steel in the concrete makes the walls impossible to drill through. Even if you *could* drill through them, it would only be possible from here, in this corridor. But here you would be seen by CCTV. As I have already mentioned, the door to the vault is over one metre thick and also made of steel-reinforced concrete, and has a dual eight-digit combination lock. Today I have one number and the duty guard has the other. These codes are also changed daily and two people always need be here to enter the two codes in order for the door to open."

Right on cue, the lift doors opened and one of the guards from the control room stepped out and walked down the corridor to join them. In the centre of the vault door was an electronic number pad with a small screen. The security guard entered his pin, then Lukas entered his. There was a long electronic beep and a hissing sound of pistons moving. De Haas turned a large handle, and the door swung effortlessly open.

Flick gazed into the vault.

Strip lights were pinging and flickering on automatically. The space inside must have been about ten metres square. The rear and right-hand walls were covered in rows of green locked doors – safety deposit boxes ranging in size and set into the concrete walls.

"Only one person is allowed in the vault at any time," said Lukas, turning to the Fox. "My friend, I feel that at this moment that person should be you."

They all stayed in the corridor and looked through the large door as the Fox entered the vault. He stepped into the space and spun round with his arms out for the cameras. Show-off, thought Flick grumpily.

Lukas said, "On the back wall are sixty small deposit boxes which pull out like drawers. The right-hand wall houses the larger boxes."

In the centre of the vault was a single two metre long glass table.

The Fox stepped forward. "And this is where the magic is going to happen," he announced dramatically.

He placed his hands on the table and closed his eyes. The camerawoman edged forwards in the doorway and lapped it up. Flick rolled her eyes. She tried to get Charlie's attention, but his head was nearly spinning as he attempted to take it all in. He seemed to be trying to look through the door in four directions at once.

"Yes," said De Haas. "After the bank closes on Friday, my diamonds will be placed in a black box in the centre of the table."

"And when you open the vault door at 9.31 p.m. they'll be gone," proclaimed the Fox with a sweep of his hands.

"If you say so," laughed De Haas. "But you should know that the vault has a heat sensor. If someone enters the vault without permission their body temperature will trigger the alarm. And if someone were to open the door, or attempt to drill through the walls, it would change the air temperature and be detected by our monitors."

The Fox walked over to the right-hand corner nearest the corridor. "This is where we will place our camera. I understand the TV crew will be able to set it up beforehand?"

"Yes. Normally we cannot open the vault during opening hours. Our insurance will not permit this. We have made an exception today just for the show, but you can only set up for the trick after the bank is closed."

"Very well," said the Fox. "Then that is what we shall do."

The camerawoman wanted to film some more material in the vault, different shots showing where the action would take place, so the security guard and the sound man stayed behind with her. The rest of them retraced their steps back down the service corridor, into the lift, and up to the ground floor.

As they travelled up in the lift the Fox hummed to himself. Flick imagined that under his mask he was looking very smug indeed.

He was getting everyone to do exactly what he wanted.

But Flick had other plans.

6
The Painting

They filmed some more shots of the Fox with Flick and Charlie outside the bank until it started to get dark, and Kevin the cameraman said they could do no more. Maybe it was the fading light, or his buttons were starting to pop off. Either way, everyone decided it was time to go home. De Haas headed further up the hill to his castle and the rest of them traipsed back to the hotel, the Fox leading the way. As they walked down through the town, they crossed a square Flick hadn't seen before. On the far side was an old wall with a huge group of tourists gathered around it taking photos.

"What's that?" asked Charlie curiously.

"It's just some old mural," said the Fox dismissively.

Charlie shot off to take a closer look and Flick followed. The Fox stopped and watched them, glancing impatiently at his watch.

There was a long series of paintings on the wall. It was hard to see all of it because of the number of people in the way, but it seemed to be telling a story about a king getting married. Flick could see that in the final picture, his bride had on a very impressive sparkly necklace.

The Fox gestured for them to get a move on and so they followed him out of the square into a much calmer side street.

"If we can pull off this trick, it will win us the competition for sure. It'll certainly grab the audience's attention. And there's one other reason you need to get into that vault." The Fox stopped and turned to face them, glancing up and down the street nervously despite the fact that they were on a quiet road lined with shops that had all shut for the day.

"In that vault is a painting," the Fox whispered. "We need to get it."

A painting. So the voice had been right.

"Why?" asked Flick, narrowing her eyes suspiciously.

"You don't need to worry about why. Just trust me. We need that painting."

He turned and started walking again and the two of them fell in behind him.

"I've worked out a method that allows us to do the trick with the diamonds *and* get the painting."

"But why do we need it?" Flick persisted.

"You don't need to know. You only need to worry about doing what I ask you," the Fox said sharply.

Charlie wrinkled his nose in confusion.

Flick wished confusion was all she felt. She was starting to get more and more angry with her mentor.

Later on, after a quick shower, Flick spotted a glossy information pamphlet by her bed informing her that the hotel offered a *premier communal dining experience for complete family enjoyment.* She was famished. Time to find out just how premier and complete her family enjoyment could be.

She left her room and walked along the corridor and slowly down the stairs. The dining room was down a short corridor from the foyer. It was a large room with about thirty tables in it, each seating four people. A waiter checked her room number as she entered. The show had taken over the hotel, and by the time Flick arrived the dining room was already full with TV and production crew. The walls were a little too white, the lighting a little too bright and the chairs a little too plastic. It didn't feel premier in the slightest.

Flick queued up. Dinner was a choice between salmon and vegetables or macaroni cheese. The macaroni looked like concrete, so Flick plumped for the salmon. After the chef had filled her plate, she looked around for somewhere to sit. She recognized a group of sound engineers at one table; another had camera crew; and then there was make-up. She wasn't sure where she could fit in.

While she was dithering, the Fox called out across the room for her to join him. Flick turned and saw him seated at a table with Kevin and some man in a suit she'd not seen before. She guessed she had no choice but to join them. Flick noticed that the Fox had no plate in front of him. He still had his fox's mask on. Did this mean that he could never eat in public? What a crazy way to live your life, she thought.

Flick put her plate on the table, pulled out a chair and sat down. While the table seated four, it was clear who was the star. The Fox was in full flow, pompously explaining how awesome he was to the man in the suit.

Flick hoped the salmon was good.

"They're type IIa," the Fox said. "That means they're in the top one per cent of the world's diamonds in terms of purity. What makes a diamond look beautiful is the amount of carbon it contains. What causes cheap diamonds to look rubbish is the level of nitrogen in them. Nitrogen makes them look yellow and nasty, but a high level of carbon makes them sparkle white. IIa diamonds have very little nitrogen in them. These are top quality, pure, very valuable stones. And there are forty-six of them in De Haas's necklace."

The man in the suit was feeding the Fox's ego, asking all the right questions. He had chosen the macaroni cheese so clearly had nothing better to do.

He asked, "What will the necklace be in, or will it just be loose on the table?"

The Fox chuckled. "You know me better than that. I've arranged for the necklace to be in a rectangular felt-lined black box, placed in the centre of the table. For the whole time that box is sitting out on display in the vault, it will be filmed by our camera. Now, the bank doesn't allow cables in or out of the vault and the walls are too thick to transmit through, so the footage of the diamonds won't be shown live. The camera will record our amazing trick onto an attached hard disk. At exactly 9.31 p.m. on Friday the vault will be opened, the diamonds will have vanished, and the hard disk will be retrieved from the camera. The recording will then be shown to Lukas."

"Wow," said the man in the suit. "So you can't drill into the bank. You can't tunnel under it. You can't dig down into it. How are you going to get in?"

The Fox laughed. "If I told you that I'd have to kill you."

Oh, please. Flick rolled her eyes and stabbed her salmon.

The Fox turned to her. "This is the girl who's going to do it. You should be asking her."

The man in the suit stared at Flick, who raised her fork in a salute. He looked doubtful. "This kid?" he asked.

Flick regretted not sitting with make-up.

"I'm training her," said the Fox. "She'll do just fine."

Suit Man asked, "Aren't you worried that others will copy

you? We could have a spate of bank robberies all across the world after your show."

"Let's just say the method involves some very special techniques."

"But you'll reveal at the end how it's all done?"

"Yes. The whole thing. No secrets. Full explanation."

"Well, I shall certainly be watching. This has to be your most outrageous stunt yet."

Flick couldn't look at the Fox. Under that mask he was almost certainly smiling.

7

The Base

After dinner, all the apprentices were told to go to reception and be filmed pretending to check in. Flick arrived as the TV crew were shooting multiple takes of the boy in the metallic blue shell suit that they had seen earlier. He had a large mop of ginger hair and kept walking in from the street through the low stone entrance, acting like he had just arrived. The boy was so short he made the door look normal sized.

Charlie appeared by Flick's side.

"Who's that?" asked Flick.

"That's Noah," Charlie replied. "He's with Synergy."

The two of them watched in silence as the crew adjusted some of the reflectors and arc lights pointing at the door, and then filmed the sequence all over again.

"Watch out," muttered Charlie.

Flick turned to see Harry and Ruby arrive. They were dressed like clones of Drake in black suits and white shirts. The bright lights made their white-blond hair and fair skin look even paler than Flick remembered. They caught Flick glancing their way, and Harry headed over to her.

Flick felt unease rising inside her. What did he want? She looked straight ahead, focusing on Noah coming through the door for what felt like the hundredth time. Out of the corner of her eye, she was aware that Harry had stopped next to Charlie.

"So, we're competing against each other again," Harry said, folding his arms.

Reluctantly Flick turned to face him. "What happened in *The Great Fox Hunt* wasn't personal."

"Oh, it was for me," muttered Harry. "And this is going to be my revenge." He turned on his heels and stalked away, back to join his sister by the stairs.

Flick looked at Charlie and rolled her eyes.

Charlie laughed. "Always so lovely to see him."

Finally the crew were satisfied with the shots of Noah, and it was the turn of Flick and Charlie. At least the lighting was correct now, so they only had to repeat the process seven times before the TV crew were happy.

"Do you want to watch Harry and Ruby film theirs?" asked Charlie.

Flick shook her head. "Nah. You can stay if you want but I've got some work to do."

She headed outside and strolled across the car park. She swiped her key card and stepped into the Team Fox base, making her way towards the Fox pod. Sitting in the pod, she put on her VR goggles and gloves. The goggles had earphones for a fully immersive experience, so she made sure these were comfortable while she looked at the screen. It said:

WELCOME TO THE FOX FILES

Anything you've ever wanted to know about magicians and their tricks, and plenty of other stuff that no one cares about but me.

Study the greats and you'll learn to be great...

How many times had Flick read those words over the last six months? *Study the greats and you'll learn to be great...* She wasn't so sure about being great, but she had spent hours at a time in this pod studying. And now she was going to try to use it to work out how her father had vanished. Last time he had just walked out on Flick and her mum. Not much of a trick there; he had just left through the front door, got in his car, driven off, and never come back. Then, in the Bahamas he had completely failed to show up. But this time he'd gone to a lot of trouble. Why had he done that? And how had he done it? Those were two big questions and Flick hoped to at least answer the how.

She clicked on a search box. There was an alphabetical list of every trick in the database, and she browsed through it looking for inspiration. She wasn't really sure where to begin. There were thousands, perhaps tens of thousands, of magic tricks and illusions available. They were listed by both the magician's name and the type of trick. And then something caught her eye – a trick she had watched weeks ago and then forgotten about.

She clicked on it and selected the option to watch a virtual performance. The screen went dark, and she found herself standing on a stage in an old theatre. It had been beautifully rendered, and by moving her feet on the pad she could walk about. Flick took in her surroundings. The wooden stage was framed by red velvet curtains and lit by powerful spotlights from a gantry above her. The detail was amazing. When she looked down, she could even see the grain in the planks of wood. And gazing out at the auditorium, Flick could see a packed virtual audience, silently waiting for the action to begin.

She walked across the stage to look at the trick she had selected. There was a lorry parked on the stage with its back doors open, and behind it, on a trailer, was a shredder. This was whirring away, ready to chop up and reduce to splinters anything that was fed into it. The shredder had a metal chute which was pointing at the back of the lorry so that all the pieces would be spat into it. Leading up to the shredder was a conveyor belt and at the far end was an open wooden coffin, the lid leaning beside it. As Flick approached the coffin, a play button appeared in front of her, so she reached out and tapped it.

A voice announced, "Ladies and gentlemen, please welcome virtual Valentino."

A dark-haired man wearing smart black trousers and a black silk shirt strode onto the stage accompanied by two assistants. He walked confidently around the far side of the coffin and climbed in. The assistants then took the lid and placed it on top. There were two holes in the lid and Valentino's hands were pulled through these and handcuffed together, preventing him from pulling them back into the coffin. Then one of the assistants produced a hammer and some nails and secured the lid in place. Valentino was now well and truly imprisoned. Next, the other assistant pulled a lever on the conveyor belt and the coffin started to glide slowly towards the shredder.

Valentino's hands waved about in distress as the coffin edged closer and closer to the shredder. But then, just as the coffin reached the shredder, his hands vanished. There was the terrible sound of splintering wood and out of the chute sprang fragments of coffin as it was smashed into tiny pieces. The audience watched in horror. Then, as the metal chute spat out the final slithers of wood, Valentino appeared through the open doors in the back of the lorry and took his bow. The audience applauded in relief.

With the trick over, the virtual spectators returned to their silent, expectant state and Flick was presented with a *How it works* button. She pressed it and a set of technical notes popped up. The shredder, the lorry and the conveyor belt were all real. The coffin was also real but had been altered in one significant way, and the handcuffs were just dummies.

It was a very dangerous trick because it relied completely on last-minute timing. As the coffin reached the end of the conveyor belt, the magician slipped the dummy handcuffs off and pulled his hands into the coffin. He then quickly opened the side of the coffin that faced away from the audience. The entire panel was hinged, allowing him to fall out behind the conveyor belt. This was hidden by some cleverly placed mirrors under the conveyor which made it look like you could see under it but, in reality, you were just seeing a reflection.

As the coffin was smashed into thousands of pieces, the magician crawled along behind the conveyor belt and the shredder and up into the cab of the lorry. He could then make his way into the back of the lorry and dramatically reappear.

Flick took her goggles off and thought about the trick. It was different from the one her dad had performed in several ways but surely there was something similar in his method. Could her dad have escaped from the wardrobe through a flap? No. There was nowhere for him to go. And all of the sides had been completely dismantled. Yet something niggled at the back of her mind. Once he had got out, he could have slipped behind the lorry…

She was too tired to think. Maybe tomorrow, when she felt fresher, she would be able to work it out. She stood up from the pod and stiffly walked to the door.

She hesitated for a moment, looking towards the fox's head logo at the back of the room.

"You were right," she said.

There was no answer.

She tried again. "You were right about the painting."

Again, nothing. She shrugged.

Exhausted, Flick made her way from the Team Fox base to her hotel room. In a daze she changed into her pyjamas and cleaned her teeth before falling into bed. She turned off the bedside lamp and lay there in the dark thinking. The voice she had heard earlier had been right: the Fox couldn't be trusted. He still wouldn't tell her anything about the Bell System or why he needed the painting, and he didn't seem at all bothered about her dad vanishing yet again. If he didn't keep his promise to help her find him, why should she help him?

She thought long and hard about the diamond trick. When she and Charlie performed it, the man in the suit from the dining room would be watching, along with everyone else. They would all see the diamonds go missing. And Flick could use that moment.

She could ruin the Great Fox's trick.

8

The Lorry

Flick woke up early the next morning with an idea. She wasn't sure where the thought had come from but during the night her mind had clearly been busy. Her dad had wanted her to see that video. It was a message to her and that meant she knew where to start looking for him. And if her hunch was right, this morning would be the perfect time to start.

She got out of bed and hopped into the shower. She had just finished putting her prosthetic leg on and getting dressed when there was a sharp knock at the door. She opened it and found Gemma there with her clipboard.

"Opening ceremony. Town centre. Now," she said curtly, and walked off briskly.

Flick checked she had her room key and then stepped out into the corridor, closing her door behind her. She knocked gently on Charlie's door.

"You coming?" she called.

There was no answer, so she knocked again. She listened but couldn't hear any noise from inside the room, so she knocked once more, this time much louder.

"Who is it?" Charlie called from inside.

"It's me. We need to go."

"Hang on."

After a few minutes, Charlie appeared. He looked tired.

"You OK?" asked Flick.

"What time is it?" he muttered.

"Early. We need to go and film the opening ceremony. And while we're there I have an idea. I was going over and over my dad's disappearing trick last night and I think I've worked it out. We need to check something."

They made their way down to the empty reception foyer.

"I think you've got your top on inside out," observed Flick.

"What?" Charlie glanced down. "Oh yes. Hang on."

Flick stepped outside and looked the other way while he undid his dungarees, removed his glasses, pulled his top over his head and put it on correctly.

"Where is everyone?" he yawned when he was done.

"Like I said, it's early."

"Exactly how early?"

"Just before six."

He rubbed his eyes. "This had better be good. Where are we going?"

"In the words of Gemma: 'Opening ceremony. Town centre. Now.' Did she not wake you up too?"

"Yeah, but I was half asleep and wasn't really listening," he confessed.

They walked up the hill through the deserted streets; none of the tourists were up yet. Even yesterday's sun was nowhere to be seen; in its place were ominous grey clouds. Eventually they arrived at the town square.

"There was a lorry here yesterday," said Flick. "They were unloading it round the back of the stage."

"Yeah, I remember seeing it."

"What's the chances of it being the lorry used in my dad's trick?"

Charlie yawned. "I would say good. How many red lorries can Channel Seven have? I've only seen the one."

They arrived at the stage. Despite the early hour, the audience was packed out with expectant fans. How much were they paying these people?

Flick and Charlie headed to the left side of the stage where there was a gate in the security fence. Gemma was waiting there and told the guard to let them through.

"They'll need to check how you look," she said to Flick.

She turned to Charlie. "And you might want to rub all that sleep dust out of your eyes."

They walked through the backstage area. Flick made sure that Gemma wasn't watching and then she pulled Charlie towards the lorry. It was parked behind another fence.

"I keep running over and over in my mind how my dad did his trick," Flick said. "He must have been hidden in one of the wooden panels that made up the wardrobe. He had to have climbed into a secret compartment. It was the only place he could have been. One of the crew had to have been in on the trick, and that crew member must have made sure he dismantled the panel my dad was in, otherwise someone would have been suspicious that it was really heavy.

"Anyway, if you remember, as they dismantled the wardrobe, some of the panels were leant against the lorry before they put them in a pile and burnt them. Well, at that moment I think my dad must have climbed out of his secret compartment and hidden behind the lorry. And I'm wondering if this was the lorry." Flick pointed through the fence at the vehicle. "Later in the trick, the lorry was used to run over the remains of the panels so Dad must have somehow hidden inside it by then."

They stared through the security fence at the lorry. It had a high sleeper cab and was painted bright red with a big number seven logo on the doors in the blue and white colours of Channel Seven.

"And I suppose," said Charlie, "you want my help in getting over this fence so you can examine that lorry?"

"What a brilliant idea," said Flick, grinning.

They looked up at the top of the fence. It must have been more than two metres high.

"Even if you climb on my shoulders, I'm not sure I'm going to get you over it," said Charlie.

"What I'm thinking," said Flick, "is that we drag one of those packing cases from the stage over here. You stand on it, and I climb on your shoulders and pull myself up over the fence. Then I'll be able to get in. But I won't be able to get back out again, so I'll need to hide in there until they start using it later. Then I guess I'll just sneak out through security."

"Or we could just walk through here," said Charlie. He pulled on a loose section of the fence, and it came away and opened like a gate.

Flick laughed. "Or that," she said as they slipped through the gap.

9
The Letter

Flick walked around the back of the lorry and down the far side towards the cab. This was where her dad would have been. He must have slipped out of his wooden panel and hidden somewhere in the lorry on this side.

And then Flick spotted it.

Underneath the front of the trailer, very near the point where it connected with the cab, was a box about three metres long. It had a long door and a small handle in the middle. She pulled on this, and it opened upwards revealing a wide space inside. Probably designed for tools or spares, it was also a perfect hiding place. Her dad would have been able to lie flat in there, shut the door, and no one would have seen him.

Flick and Charlie crouched down and peered inside. It

smelt of oil and there were some spanners in a pile at one end. And there on the back wall was a note, stuck on with a bit of tape. Flick reached in and grabbed it, pulling it out into the light.

Dear Flick,

Well done for finding this! I'm sorry I still can't be with you. I always tried to teach you to take ownership of your mistakes and that is what I am trying to do.

Flick stared at the note. For the first time in as long as she could remember, she held something from her father. A thing that he had written, and touched, and placed in this spot. For her. He had reached out *just* to her. Finally.

She read it again.

And again.

This proved she was on the right track.

"What does it say?" asked Charlie.

Flick passed it to him, and he read it in silence while Flick stared at the empty compartment. Her father had been right there in that space. Not long ago.

She reached out and ran her hand along the floor.

When Charlie finished reading, he said, "Is that it?"

"What do you mean?"

"Well, it's not the longest letter from a father to a daughter, is it?"

"I'm so close, Charlie. This proves it."

"But he's not asking you to look for him, or help him, or—"

"We're not stopping now, Charlie. We're so close. Listen, this is my dad. Would you give up if this was your dad? Or your brother?"

"He hardly says anything. I'd—"

"I will not stop. Never. You can either help me or not."

"Do you even think your dad wrote this? I…"

But Flick was already walking towards the gap in the fence. "I know he was here. And I remember from the video where the lorry ended up, and that must have been where he slipped out of his hiding place. It stopped right in front of a green door in what looks like a tower, and I bet we'll find that tower in the castle. When the lorry was parked, he must have quietly climbed out and slipped through the door into the tower. That's where we need to go and look next. Are you coming?"

"What about the opening ceremony," protested Charlie, hurrying after her. "Shouldn't we wait till that's over?"

As Flick and Charlie stepped back through the fence, Gemma spotted them.

"Act like we got a bit lost," Flick whispered to Charlie as Gemma stormed towards them with a scowl on her face.

"How do you two manage to be late for everything?" she growled.

"Sorry," said Charlie. "We ended up in the wrong place and then we didn't know how to get out and then we saw the hole in the fence and that meant—"

Gemma held up her hand. "I'm not interested in your boring little life, Charlie. Just get up on that stage right now."

"We will," said Flick meekly, and the two of them headed back towards the stage.

Flick slowly climbed the stairs, and they were ushered into the wings. Flick's mind was spinning with her discovery. She was so close on her father's trail – she couldn't be far behind him. She was struggling to remember the details of his face. It had been over a year now since she had last seen him, and her memory was fading. She wasn't sure if the image she had of him in her head was accurate. How tall was he? How deep was his voice? Her mum had been struggling more and more. She put on a brave face while they were in the Bahamas, but Flick could tell she was sad and lonely without him. Even though her mum had tried to persuade her to stop looking for him, Flick knew she didn't really mean it. Flick was determined to find him and bring him home.

And there was something else, nagging at the back of Flick's mind. Her father had left her a note in a hidden location. He hadn't given it to the Fox to pass on to her. He hadn't trusted the Fox with it. This was surely further proof that Flick couldn't trust the Fox either. The more she thought about it, the more certain she became.

In the wings Flick and Charlie found themselves standing next to the magician from Synergy. He had a wide smile and was wearing his usual metallic blue shell suit, and Flick thought he looked even taller close up. With him was Noah, also wearing his shell suit. The magician beamed maniacally at Flick.

"So lovely to meet the great Flick Lions," he said, offering her his hand. Flick took it cautiously and immediately felt him palm her a card. He gave her a wink and then turned back to face the stage.

Flick peeped at the card in her hand. It said:

Synergy.

Where the magic happens.

Underneath he had written a phone number and a note which read:

We need to talk!

Onstage they were playing a pre-recorded backstory for each of the four teams. For Team Fox, they showed a couple of minutes of their stay in the Bahamas and the training the Fox had been giving them. There were shots of Flick in a Fox pod learning methods, and then Flick practising a performance with Charlie. Running through it again and again until each trick was perfect.

They really were a great team, Flick thought.

Finally, the film ended and Christina started to ramp up the excitement. "So how would you like to meet the contestants?" she shouted into her microphone.

A thumping bass pounded from the speakers.

"First up, we have Winston from Synergy and his apprentice, Noah!"

The pair stepped out onto the stage and saluted the crowd, beaming.

"Next up, we have Dominic Drake with his apprentices, Harry and Ruby!"

The crowd cheered as from the other side of the stage Drake, Harry and Ruby appeared. Drake hadn't lost any of his swagger and his hair and beard looked less grey than Flick remembered. He was wearing his usual black suit with a green pocket handkerchief that matched his eyes and was carrying his trademark silver cane. And he'd clearly been shopping because Harry and Ruby had on matching outfits. The three of them stood in a line, all leaning on their canes, looking like they were about to break out in a song and dance routine.

"And now," continued Christina, "please put your hands together for … the Great Fox and his apprentices, Flick and Charlie!"

A stagehand signalled and Flick, Charlie and the Fox stepped forward. Flick tried to look out at the audience, but the bright lights meant it was impossible to see beyond the first row. The Fox and Charlie waved but Flick decided to keep her joy in check.

"And last but not least, can we have a big welcome for the Studio Three Crew with apprentice Saanvi!"

From the opposite wings a man with a shaved head and wearing a dark blue shirt, jeans and large white-rimmed sunglasses walked on. With him was a girl with long black hair; she was wearing blue jeans and a bright pink T-shirt.

"These are our four mentors and their apprentices. Give them all a huge round of applause!"

The audience cheered and clapped wildly.

"These four teams will compete for the chancellorship of the Global Order of Magic over two rounds. At the end of the first round, two teams will be eliminated, leaving the two remaining teams to battle it out in the final. In the first round, the apprentices will have to create and perform a magic trick with no help from their mentor, and the apprentices from another team will be randomly selected to try to work out their method. The slowest two teams to work out their trick will leave the competition. The teams that make it through to the second and final round will be invited to perform the best trick they can come up with, this time with the help of their mentor."

Christina spun round to face a camera that had joined her onstage. She beamed into the lens. "All that remains is for me to declare this competition open."

Fireworks shot up on either side of the stage and the big screen behind them went crazy with stars and sparkles. The music thumped and the cheers of the crowd became deafening.

"Let the magic begin!"

PART TWO

Discoveries

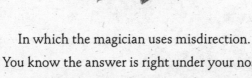

In which the magician uses misdirection.
You know the answer is right under your nose,
but the magician cleverly distracts you
and throws you off the scent.

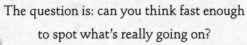

The question is: can you think fast enough
to spot what's really going on?

10
The Practice

The next morning, Flick got up at seven, dressed as quickly as she could, and headed downstairs to receive the Fox's instructions. These had been left in an envelope on a table in the ballroom. Now the competition had officially started, the Fox and the other mentors were no longer allowed to remain in Linth, but they were permitted to leave their apprentices information on what they should do for their final trick. If Flick and Charlie managed to get through the first round, this would be the important one.

Flick walked into the ballroom, a very long room with a little stage at one end and miles of polished wooden floor. The other teams were using their bases, but this room gave Team Fox the space they needed to practise their grand finale.

Several large chandeliers hung from the ceiling, and down one wall there were a series of grand arched windows. She found a trestle table in front of the stage with a sign on it which said *Team Fox*. In the middle of the table was an envelope with a package. She rubbed her tired eyes and tore open the envelope. Several sheets of paper spilt out. The Fox had not held back on details. She riffled through the pages, fixing the outline of the whole thing in her mind.

Their final trick. It would be amazing, but it would require an intense practice routine.

The Fox's plan was for Flick and Charlie to start working on this trick before worrying about the trick for the first round, which could be much more straightforward. It was a good plan, assuming they made it into the last round and assuming it wasn't too complicated for Flick to learn.

She slowly read through the instructions again. As was usual in their partnership, Charlie was going to play a supporting role, and she was going to have to do all the hard parts, of which there were many. She would be spending a *lot* of time practising. But what a trick! She got goosebumps as she lingered on the details, a grin spreading across her face. If they pulled it off, it would be the best trick she had ever performed by a million miles. Whatever else the Fox was, he was a genius magician.

She pulled the package towards her and opened it. Inside were some black overalls similar to the ones worn by Channel

Seven's TV crew. According to the Fox's instructions, she would need to wear these for the trick. Flick decided to slip back up to her room and try them on straight away.

The overalls had full-length trousers, so Flick found getting her prosthetic into them a bit of a struggle. But on the other hand, they were nice and baggy, so once she'd put them on, they fitted well. Satisfied, Flick decided to keep them on and headed back downstairs to breakfast.

The dining room was just as busy and noisy in the mornings. There was no sign of Charlie, but this time Flick managed to sit with a couple of people from the sound department. They were, thankfully, very quiet. Maybe if you spend all your day dealing with sound you need a bit of time off from it, she mused.

After breakfast, she made her way back to the ballroom, where she was pleased to see Charlie had turned up. This was where the real work began. The Fox had instructed them to practise, practise and practise.

"There are so many instructions," commented Charlie, examining the pages. "It's an incredibly hard trick, but it will be absolutely amazing, if we can make it work."

Flick folded her arms. "You say if *we* can make it work, but have you seen how many of those instructions actually apply to you?"

"Um… Just the section about the timer."

"And how long is that section?"

"One sentence."

Flick turned to look at their props.

The Fox had arranged for a glass table to be placed in the ballroom, on which sat a black rectangular box. Both the table and the box were identical to the ones that would be in the bank vault. Inside the practice box was a replica necklace with forty-six glass diamonds, nearly the same as the real necklace in weight and feel. Behind this practice box was a second black box, identical in every way except for one crucial detail: it did not contain any diamonds. Each box was thirteen centimetres long, seven centimetres wide and four centimetres deep. They were made of plastic, covered in black leather, and lined with black felt. Flick's job was to practise switching the one containing the diamonds with the one without. Charlie just had to prepare the contents of this second box.

"Did you see that the timer in the second box has to be set to just before half past nine on Friday night?" Charlie asked, fiddling with the box. "Well, nine twenty-nine to be precise. It's very specific, which suggests you need to be very accurate with the timing of what you do."

"No pressure then," muttered Flick.

She read through the instructions again and again while Charlie carefully placed a small black object in his box. After a couple of minutes, he placed the box on the table and folded his arms triumphantly.

"Is that you done?" asked Flick.

He nodded happily. "I believe that's it."

"So, I have to work out how to perform this very complicated set of moves and you just have to start a timer?"

Charlie smirked. "You're the magician; I'm just the talented creative inventor."

"Remind me what you've recently invented," Flick said drily as she started to go through the moves for the first time.

The key to the trick was that the switch had to be invisible from the front, so Flick needed to perform the move with her back to the table and the diamonds. This was where her black overalls came in. In the centre of her back was a pouch designed to be big enough to contain the box of diamonds. This was made out of the same material as the rest of the overalls, so was invisible.

"Let's have it then," ordered Flick.

Charlie picked the second box up again and passed it to her, and she placed it in the hidden pouch.

The first thing Flick needed to practise was standing facing away from the table and reaching behind with her hands to feel for the diamonds. She then pulled the full box across the table, towards her bum. Next, she removed Charlie's box from its hiding place in her pouch. She pushed it up from the bottom of the pouch, just enough so her fingers could grab the top as it peeped out of the cloth, careful not to let it fall out onto the floor. Then with her other hand she took hold of the lid and gently pulled it all the way out of the pouch and placed Charlie's box on the table, next to the real one. There were now two black boxes on the table behind her, one full of diamonds and one containing Charlie's timer. Next, she picked up the real box and slid it into her pouch. The two boxes had now been switched.

It was a long and complicated series of movements, but if everything went to plan Flick would only have around fifteen seconds to perform this element of the trick. The hardest part was reaching behind her to find the real box. To cover this action, Flick decided she would pretend to stretch. By massaging her left shoulder with her right hand and then arching her left arm as if she was stretching it behind her, the movement could be made to seem like she was performing an exercise to counteract a bit of shoulder pain.

She ran through the sequence again while Charlie watched. Then she tried it a third time.

"How's your brother?" Flick asked while midway through the process.

"He's the same. No better, but also no worse. It's depressing that nothing seems to change; they try lots of different treatments, but he never improves. The doctors recently tried some more deep brain stimulation but that didn't make any difference, and I've lost count of how many times they've tried it before. After a while you sort of stop hoping, because you don't want to be disappointed when whatever it is they're currently trying doesn't work. It's like his life is stuck on a loop, repeating over and over but never changing or getting any better."

Flick paused and looked at Charlie. "I'm sorry," she said quietly. "I really am."

He shrugged. "There's nothing any of us can do. You of all people know how important patience is."

Flick nodded sympathetically. "It's hard." She put the boxes down and walked over to Charlie. Then she did something she rarely ever did. She hugged him.

Charlie's glasses were knocked skew-whiff by the hug, and he resettled them on his nose. "Thank you," he said, looking pleased. "And you've reminded me that I ought to video call my parents and see how they are. I'll leave you to practise."

He hurried out of the ballroom and Flick was left alone. She continued practising, swapping the boxes again and again. By the time she'd run through the sequence fifty times, she had all the details worked out. She was starting to feel mentally tired from all the concentration when Gemma arrived. She stood in the doorway and frowned at her clipboard.

"You need to be in the great hall of the castle in an hour. It's your turn in the hot seats to see one of the other teams' first trick," she announced. "And you'll need to leave soon because you're so slow at walking."

Don't beat around the bush, thought Flick, and nodded briefly, but Gemma had already left without waiting for her response.

Flick allowed herself another fifteen minutes of practice. For the last ten repetitions, she completed the sequence in about seven seconds. There was a laptop set up in the corner of the room which they were allowed to use to email the Fox, so she sent him a message explaining how quickly she'd been able to perform the switch. She hoped he would be impressed.

What she didn't tell him was the little addition she was planning. At the end of the trick, if all went to plan, the diamonds would be shown to have disappeared, and then they would be shown reappearing in a different location. But Flick was planning her own little surprise. When it came to the crucial moment, she wasn't going to make the switch. When the box in the vault was inspected at the grand climax – the Fox's big reveal – the diamonds would still be there. The Great Lion was going to teach the Great Fox a lesson.

11

The Great Hall

Flick left the hotel and made her way up the hill towards the castle. It was an impressive structure, perched high on a large rock overlooking the town. Linth seemed to live in its shadow. She climbed higher and higher past shops and houses as the road got steeper, catching glimpses of the castle between the gaps in the buildings. At times she could see a tower; at other times only the walls were visible.

Eventually Flick arrived at the base of the crag the castle was built on. Here the road was cut into the side of the rock and zigzagged its way up. She puffed onwards up the steep tarmac road in the heat of the day. Finally, at the top, she got to the castle walls, which she followed round to a set of large iron gates.

Pausing for breath, Flick stopped to take in the view below. Looking out over the tiled roofs, she could see the narrow streets, the bank and the hotel, and all the way down to the waterfront. She turned one hundred and eighty degrees and looked up at the castle. The high ramparted wall stretched off in both directions from the gates, and beyond that she could make out the top of the round tower and the keep.

She stepped through the open gates and found herself in a large stone courtyard. There was the round tower on the right-hand side, and directly ahead was the entrance to the keep. Flick could see Charlie standing by the large wooden door, so she crossed the courtyard towards him.

"Are you ready for this?" he asked eagerly.

"Not really. I've got more important things to do," muttered Flick.

There were a couple of shallow stone steps leading up to the entrance, which Flick didn't find too challenging, and inside was a long narrow hallway with a red carpet down the centre. On both sides, suits of armour were displayed. The first knight held a pike and the next a spear, and their armour gleamed under spotlights set into the ceiling. Down the hallway on the left was a wooden staircase, but Flick and Charlie followed the large sign directing them into the great hall through a low stone entrance on their right.

It was quite a room: about thirty metres long and ten metres wide, and completely dominated by wood. There was a wooden floor, wooden panelling on the walls, a wooden stage at the far end, a wooden balcony on the opposite wall and a long wooden banqueting table in the middle. With wooden chairs. After they'd finished decorating, there couldn't have been many trees left in the area, Flick thought.

Christina was already up on the stage while the TV crew bustled around her. They had constructed lighting gantries on the ceiling and they had hung four flags as a backdrop to the stage, in a nod to their medieval surroundings. There was one with a fox's head on it for their team, another with a three of clubs for the Studio Three Crew, one with a lightning bolt for Synergy and the fourth had a silver cane for Dominic Drake.

As soon as members of the TV crew spotted Charlie and Flick, they beckoned them onto the stage. Christina sat down in a chair, and Flick and Charlie plonked themselves in two more chairs facing her. Beside her was a large screen.

Someone shouted "Action!" and Christina instantly leant forward and gazed earnestly at them.

"Charlie and Flick, welcome to the hot seats," she said with a furrowed brow. "This is where things start to heat up. For this first round of the competition, we're going to play you a film of the Studio Three Crew's trick, and you will need to come back here tonight and tell us how the trick was done."

The screen showed a film of Saanvi, wearing blue jeans and a bright orange T-shirt, walking down one of the main streets in Linth. She was being filmed by a slightly wobbly handheld camera that zoomed in on her face as she approached a family of tourists, a mum and dad with a young boy and an older girl.

"Hey, guys, would you like to see a trick?" she asked, waving a pack of cards at them. "I'm part of this magic competition going on in town and I'd love to try something."

The family smiled and nodded. Why wouldn't they want to see some street magic?

Saanvi riffled through the cards and cut the deck twice. She fanned the cards out face up.

"Can you see the cards are all mixed up?"

The family agreed. They were in a random order.

"Now, I'm going to give you the cards." Saanvi placed the deck in the hands of the mum. "And I'd like *you*," she said to the dad, "to hold your hand palm up." She turned back to Mum. "Can you cut a portion of the cards and place them face down on his hand?"

Mum did just that.

Saanvi then took the remaining cards from Mum. "Now, you placed some of the cards in his hand." She fanned out the rest of the cards. "So, from these remaining cards, I would like you to pick one."

The mum chose a card.

"Let everybody see it."

The mum showed it to her family and to the camera while Saanvi turned away.

"OK, now we'll put your card back in your section of the pile." Saanvi cut the mum's cards and the chosen card was returned to the deck. She then gave them back to Mum to hold, and turned to the son. "Do you know what an indicator card is?" she asked.

The boy shook his head.

"It's something that a card player might use. For example, they might place a four in the deck, and they know that four cards away from it is the ace. It's a way of keeping track of where cards are."

The boy nodded in understanding.

"So, this pile" – Saanvi pointed at the portion still sitting face down on the dad's hand – "is the indicator pile. Please take those cards, and then I want you to deal them one at a time back onto your dad's hand. And wherever you choose to stop, that card will indicate the position of your mum's card in her pile."

The boy nodded again. "OK."

He slowly dealt a few cards onto his dad's hand.

"Now, when you stop, I'm going to ask if you want to change your mind, because I don't want you to think I've made you stop there. OK? Remember, your card will indicate where your mum's card is in the other pile."

The boy stopped dealing cards.

"You've chosen to stop. Do you want to change your mind? Deal more cards? Or take some back?"

The boy laughed, hesitated and then took two cards back.

"OK, let's look at the card."

Saanvi turned over the top card. It was the nine of clubs.

"So, if you had taken one more card it would have been a…" She turned over the next card. "A two. And if you had taken one less card…" She turned this over to reveal a king. "But you chose the nine of clubs."

Saanvi looked at the mum. "OK, so deal out nine cards, please."

The mum counted eight cards onto Saanvi's palm. When she got to the ninth Saanvi said to the boy, "Remember, you could have stopped at any point. You chose the nine of clubs. OK, now turn over the ninth card."

The mum turned it over and her card was revealed. The family of tourists stared at it open-mouthed.

Saanvi grinned.

12
The Castle

After watching the trick, Flick and Charlie were dismissed, so they made their way down the steps and across the great hall. The TV crew were removing the wooden banqueting table and filling the room with plastic chairs, so they had to weave their way around the furniture to reach the hallway.

"While we're here, there's something I'm desperate to check," Flick whispered. "Follow me."

"The trick Saanvi did was seriously cool, wasn't it?" said Charlie.

Flick shrugged, only half listening. "It was all right."

"I mean, she's just effortlessly stylish," he continued undeterred. "And her hair is so shiny; it catches the light and gives her such an aura." He gazed into the distance.

"Wow. I actually have sick in my mouth."

"Well, I thought it was pretty cool. But what sort of trick do you think we should do? I can't decide what will best play to the television audience. We need either a really good close-up trick or a large-scale illusion. Sometimes a close-up can work really well on TV but maybe we should go big and make a—"

Flick interrupted him. "This is your department; you're the talented creative inventor, remember?"

"The problem is I have *loads* of ideas. I was just wondering what style of trick we want to perform. We could go with a vanishing trick, or a card trick... Oh, and I was thinking it would be really—"

He stopped. Flick looked up to see Charlie standing dead still, seemingly utterly fascinated by a suit of armour. What was he doing?

Oh. Saanvi had walked through the castle entrance and was coming down the hallway towards them. Today she was wearing a dayglo green T-shirt.

"Hey, Flick," she called. "Hi, Charlie."

Charlie examined the plaque by the suit of armour as if his life depended on it.

"Hi, Saanvi," Flick said.

"What are you guys up to today?" Saanvi asked.

"Oh, you know," said Flick. "This and that."

"I'm working on my final trick today," said Saanvi. "Studio Three want me to get it perfect but I'm struggling.

If I can get it right it will be amazing, but it's so difficult."

"Well, we mustn't be keeping you," said Flick politely, moving past her. "Come on, Charlie."

"Oh. Hi, Saanvi," said Charlie, simultaneously looking up and trying to lean nonchalantly against the plaque.

Flick rolled her eyes. "We've done that bit," she murmured, grabbing him by the arm. "Come on."

Flick managed to steer Charlie past Saanvi down the hallway towards the entrance, his face fixed in an inane grin.

"What's the matter with you?" hissed Flick as they stepped outside into the sunshine.

"Nothing," said Charlie.

"Why did you turn into such a weirdo when Saanvi turned up?"

"I was fine."

Flick shook her head. "OK then, let's get back to business. I need to find my dad. At the end of the film, the lorry was parked in front of the door to that tower over there. That must have been for a reason."

Charlie looked awkward. "Don't you think we should concentrate on the competition?" he asked quietly.

Flick paused. "You're right. We do need to win the competition to keep the Bell System safe, not to help the Fox become chancellor."

"But if he becomes chancellor the Bell System *will* be safe."

"According to him."

"Don't you believe him?"

"Well, he conveniently gets what he wants, which is to become chancellor."

"Doesn't make him wrong."

"And it just so happens he needs our help to become chancellor. Bit of a coincidence, isn't it? The whole point of *The Great Fox Hunt* must have been to get us here. Even you agreed he must have recruited us knowing this was coming. It's all been about him getting what he wants from the start."

"Maybe. But I believe him when he says he's trying to stop the Bell System from falling into the wrong hands. I believe him when he says he's trying to help your dad. I believe him when he says the best way to do that is to win this competition."

"Well, I don't."

"Let's say we put this to one side for now, and focus on trying to work out how Saanvi did her trick. We have to give our answer this evening."

Flick sighed. "We do. So we need to split up, concentrate on what we're good at. You focus on creating the trick we'll perform for the first round this afternoon; I'll concentrate on practising for the Fox's trick in the final round. But first we need to take a quick look at that tower."

"But what about Saanvi's—"

But Flick had already set off across the courtyard. To her left was the part of the castle where the De Haas family still lived.

Dotted about were some information boards, including one about a tour; further on was a low building that looked like it might house the tearoom and gift shop. There was a large group of tourists exiting it, no doubt stocking up on key rings, but what Flick was really interested in was even further along the wall. In one corner was a large round tower, and at the base was a dark green door with small windows at various heights up the wall which Flick guessed followed a staircase. At the top was a red-tiled roof.

Reluctantly following her, Charlie spotted the information boards and gleefully made a beeline towards them.

"We don't have time to be tourists," Flick muttered over her shoulder.

"I'll catch you up," Charlie called back.

"You're just taking advantage of how slow I am," Flick retorted.

By the time she had reached the tower, Charlie was with her.

"Keep it short," said Flick without taking her eyes off the green door.

"Basically, the castle has been owned by a lot of people called Ludwig."

"Is that it?"

"Pretty much. Inside the castle is a collection of capes belonging to Charles the Bold, and there was a lot of information about various types of local cheeses, and then there was a—"

"OK!" Flick interrupted. "Look, this is the spot where my dad ended his trick."

"Do you think I could get away with calling myself Charles the Bold?"

"He chose to do it right in front of this door. Now, the question is, why? What is so special about this door?"

"What if I wore a cape?"

"If you can get us through this door, you can wear whatever you like."

They stood and looked at the door.

"There's a keypad to unlock it," Charlie pointed out.

"I've noticed that."

"So we're going to need the code."

"Not really earning the cape so far."

"Or we get someone to open the door for us."

"OK. But how?"

"We knock on it, and then when someone answers the door, we ask them something stupid, like, where is the entrance to the castle, and they'll point to where the huge door is over there, and then we thank them and they close the door. But as it closes, we wedge something in the door so it doesn't fully shut."

"I don't think that's going to... Actually, that isn't the worst idea you've ever come up with. What can we put in the door?"

"Something thin, like a credit card."

"Have you got one?"

"No."

"Hmm," Flick said, turning to watch another group of tourists crossing the courtyard towards the keep entrance. "And we'd also need to get through the door unobserved. Maybe at night? But at night the courtyard is locked. So we're no further forward…"

Flick trailed off. Her eye was caught by a woman dressed all in black. She was wearing a green apron and carrying a teapot, a cup and a covered plate on a wooden tray. Flick guessed she was a member of the tearoom staff. The direction the woman was heading in could only mean one thing: she was going into the tower. Unless she was bringing tea and cake to Charlie and Flick, which seemed unlikely.

Flick angled herself so she could see the keypad without arousing the woman's suspicion.

"Charlie, look like a dim tourist," she hissed.

"What?"

"That's perfect."

Reaching the door, the woman balanced the tray in her left hand while she typed the pin in with her right. Flick watched carefully out of the corner of her eye.

She waited for the woman to pass through the door and for it to shut behind her, then edged closer, trying to look as casual as possible. The waitress had pressed three keys in a diagonal line from top right to bottom left. An easy pattern to remember.

"I make it three–five–seven," said Flick.

"We should get you the cape," said Charlie.

"Let's worry about my cape later. For now, let's take a leaf out of my dad's book," said Flick. "What we need is a big distraction."

13
The Promise

Charlie spent the long walk back down the hill trying to work out how Saanvi had done her trick.

"First she gets the woman to place some cards into the man's hand," he said. "She has no control over how many. Then the woman picks a card from those that are left. That looks a fair choice. Then Saanvi puts that card into the rest of the pack and gives it back to the woman. So from this moment the trick must be done, because she doesn't touch the cards again."

Flick ignored him. She was spending the walk thinking about how best to create a distraction. Or trying to.

"The question is," Charlie continued, "how does Saanvi know where the indicator card points to? How can she control that card?"

Flick kept walking in silence, turning possibilities over and over in her mind.

"I know you want to find your dad," Charlie persisted, "but will you promise me you'll think about this trick?"

Flick waved her hand. "Of course."

"Working out other people's tricks is definitely one of your skills. Promise me you'll help me solve this before we have to give our answer tonight?"

"Promise."

They spent the rest of the walk in silence, each thinking through their different problems. By the time they passed the fountain and entered the hotel, Flick thought she had cracked hers. Every team in the competition had to perform a first-round trick. Saanvi had already performed hers, but there were still three tricks to film, including their own. What better distraction could there be?

Inside, they were met by Gemma and her trusty clipboard. She scowled at Flick.

"You're late for your video call home," Gemma grumbled, tapping her schedule crossly. "You're supposed to call your parents or guardians every day."

Flick shrugged. "I've been busy."

"Then do it now. They're waiting for you in the video room. And I assume you've worked out by now where you will be filming your first trick, because the crew need to set up the cameras beforehand."

Flick turned to Charlie. "I think for our first-round trick this afternoon we need to perform a big illusion up at the castle and you need to take the lead. I'll meet you in our HQ after I've spoken to Mum and we'll go over the details."

Charlie raised his eyebrows and looked at her over his glasses, but he didn't argue.

Flick headed down the corridor past the ballroom. Coming towards her, having just left the video room, were Harry and Ruby.

Flick gave a smile. "Hi, Harry; hi, Ruby."

"Hi, Flick," said Ruby. Harry just glared at her.

The video room contained a comfy armchair positioned directly in front of a camera and a screen. On the screen was a guy from the TV crew wearing a headset, sitting at a desk.

"Hi, Felicity. Welcome to the video room. Make yourself comfortable. We have your mum waiting for you. We'll connect you now."

The screen went black and then a different man appeared. He was wearing a bright metallic blue shell suit.

"Hello, Flick," he said.

Flick stared at him. "Winston. What are you doing?"

The man laughed. "I'm sorry to hijack your call home, although you've got to admit it's a pretty cool trick. Anyway, I appreciate you want to talk to your mum, so I won't keep you long. I just wanted to say that we at Synergy have been watching your progress with some interest. You have a natural talent. You're already a good magician; with our help you could be a great one. We'd love to work with you."

"But I'm one of the Great Fox's apprentices," she pointed out.

"We know. But he wants us to work together."

"Really? So why hasn't he said anything to me about this? I'm not going to switch sides."

"It wouldn't involve changing sides. We just need to work together here to defeat a common enemy."

"No. I'm with Charlie, and we go back a long—"

"Charlie could join us as well if you wanted. Although we're mainly interested in you."

"Thank you, but I don't think so."

"You want to find your dad, don't you? Well, the sooner we join forces, the quicker you'll get to see him."

"You know where he is?" Flick said, startled.

"Well…" Winston laughed. "If you join us, we can take you to him."

Flick sat in silence and stared at him. First the voice and now Synergy claiming to know where her dad was. What on earth was going on?

"At least think about it, yes?"

Before she could reply, the screen went black then her mum appeared.

"That was strange," her mother said. "It was like I couldn't get through for a minute, and then it all went black. Not sure what happened there."

Were Synergy and whoever was behind the voice working together? Could they be trusted? Flick's mind was a confused mess, but she tried to smile for her mum.

"Sorry," she said. "I think there were some technical problems."

"So, how is the competition going?" her mum asked excitedly.

Flick took a deep breath and tried to calm her nerves. "Well, for the first round each team has to perform a trick, and Charlie and I are performing ours this afternoon up at the castle. Let's just say we're going to use the whole thing as a giant bit of misdirection..."

14
The Door

Later that afternoon, Charlie stood in the castle courtyard and waited for the signal to begin. He paced up and down nervously, going over the details in his head one more time. Their survival in the competition depended on the next few minutes, so he needed to do a good job. There could be no mistakes.

The TV crew had attached a camera to a very big boom. This meant it could show the inside of the castle walls, and as the trick progressed, it could slowly rise up over the top of the ramparts, and then down the other side, to film the outside too. He watched as the operator practised this move one more time, moving the camera in a slow arc. Half a dozen assistants, all dressed in black, were standing nearby. Everyone was ready.

Charlie closed his eyes and took a deep breath. He paused for a few seconds before opening his eyes and exhaling.

Time to begin.

The assistants wheeled two raised platforms up to the castle walls: one inside the courtyard and one outside on the zigzag road. Each platform had a roof held up by four vertical poles forming an open-sided cube. Some steps were wheeled up to the platform on the inside and Charlie climbed them. He stood on the platform and examined the stonework, demonstrating to the camera that the wall was solid. He then came back down the steps and waited while some rigid white blinds were placed all around the platform by the assistants. Next, a bright spotlight was switched on behind the blinds. The light could be seen shining through the translucent material.

Charlie went back up the steps and ducked under the blinds onto the platform. His shadow could clearly be seen as he walked across the platform and up to the wall. The steps were wheeled away. The silhouette of Charlie reached towards the wall and the camera captured the moment his shadow passed into it.

A moment later, the blinds were removed by the assistants and the platform was revealed to be empty. Charlie had vanished into the wall.

Flick, dressed in her black overalls and indistinguishable from the other assistants, was in the group that stepped forward and tore down the blinds. She carried one of them out of shot and propped it up next to the door of the tower. The other assistants passed her their blinds and she stacked them in the same place, creating a screen. Then she ducked down behind the blinds and entered the pin code. The door opened with a satisfying click, and she stepped inside.

Flick found herself in a stairwell. On the left was a stone spiral staircase and on the right were a couple of wooden doors. She tentatively nudged these open. The first led into a very small toilet. The second was a little kitchen, complete with a kettle, a sink and a fridge.

Flick closed the kitchen door and paused, looking up at the stairs. She sighed. Why were answers always upstairs? Why could life not supply all its helpful information at ground level?

She tackled the steps as she always did. Slowly. With both feet on each step before attempting the next. Up the spiral staircase she went, following the curved wall of the tower. She kept going. Higher and higher. There were no other floors. Occasionally there was just a larger step, a bigger bit of stone, and there were small windows to let in the light. But nothing else. Just endless steps.

Flick had been climbing for several minutes when she heard a noise. She stopped to listen. There it was again. It was clearly the sound of a door closing and then footsteps.

The noise was coming from further up the stairs.

Flick froze.

Outside the tower, the camera on the boom soared over the wall, following Charlie's passage through the solid structure. On the other side, the steps were wheeled up to the second platform and the blinds were attached. A spotlight was switched on and Charlie's silhouette appeared, coming out of the wall. When the blinds were removed, he was standing in the middle of the platform with a huge grin on his face.

He had successfully disappeared, passed through a solid wall, and reappeared.

Inside the tower, Flick listened to the approaching footsteps. They were fast, as if the person was well practised at descending the staircase. And they were getting ever closer.

She looked around.

There was nowhere to hide.

15
The Office

Flick's only choice was to climb back down the stairs as fast as possible. Rather than putting her prosthetic onto each step and then her good leg, placing both feet carefully before tackling the next, she would have to take them at full stretch. This would involve landing with her full weight on her prosthetic, and also repeatedly bending at that knee.

This was going to hurt.

Flick lengthened her stride and winced at the impact on her limb. Every step jolted up through her leg and with each bend of the knee she could feel the end of her limb getting hotter and turning raw.

She bumped her way down as fast as she could. At the bottom, she ran to the kitchen door, yanked it open, slipped inside and pulled it closed behind her. The person coming down the steps was very close now; she could hear them just around the corner, so she didn't pull the door completely shut, in case it clicked. Had they heard her? She hadn't exactly been quiet. Even her heavy breathing seemed to reverberate around the tiny kitchen, so she held her breath.

She waited.

Flick heard a door open. She risked a glance out into the stairwell and saw the arm of a silk shirt pull the green door shut. It looked like Lukas. He'd somehow not heard her. And he'd left the tower.

She let out her breath and stood motionless in the kitchen for a minute. That had been close. Too close. Should she continue? She had come this far, she reasoned. She was doing what had to be done. She had to press on. And so, she left the kitchen and slowly started to climb the stairs again.

Her limb was really hurting now. Each step was a spike of pain. She knew the sensible thing to do would be to stop and rest, but there was no going back now.

At last she arrived at the top and found a landing with a single door. Flick gently pulled it open and peeped in. The room was empty, so she stepped inside.

It was clearly Lukas's office. There was a large desk and behind it, covering the whole wall, was a bookcase. The desk was empty apart from a laptop. Under the right-hand side was a drawer, and behind it was a high-backed leather chair.

Flick sat in the chair. Where should she start? She looked around. On the wall opposite her, next to the door she had come through, was a large painting of the castle and a sunset in the background. In front of her was the desk, and she looked down and pulled the drawer open. Inside she found some pens, a stapler, some spare batteries and an elastic band. Under these were some old books on sleight of hand and under *these* was a folded-up piece of paper. Flick eased it out and spread it carefully across the desk. It was an old map of Linth, a bit yellow round the edges and clearly well used. Someone had scribbled some notes on the left-hand side which were hard to read. On the map Flick could make out the castle, the hotel, the bank and the waterfront, along with the town square and the church. But what caught her eye was a dotted line drawn on the map. The line led from the castle keep to the fountain in the square outside the hotel.

Flick tried to decipher the handwritten notes. They appeared to outline some sort of trick. The magician would stand outside the hotel on a platform in front of the fountain. A curtain would be raised, and he would quickly jump off the back of the stage and through some sort of door near the fountain. The dotted line appeared to show a tunnel leading all the way to the castle. In the great hall would be a second platform and he would then climb up the back of this stage and reappear.

Flick thought about this for a moment. It was an interesting trick, but it wouldn't be very impressive if the magician didn't reappear quickly. If he had to walk for ages along a hidden pathway all the way uphill to the castle, it would be an extremely slow process, and therefore not a very good trick. Flick wondered what else the dotted line might represent.

She folded the map and tucked it back in the drawer, and paused for a moment or two, staring at the painting in front of her. The painting was at a slight angle. The way it hung nagged at her, so she got up and walked around the desk to look more closely. She lifted the corner of the painting and took a peek behind it. Sure enough, in the centre was the door to a wall safe. Flick carefully lifted the painting down from its hook and examined the lock. It was a keypad – same layout as the door to the tower. Surely De Haas wouldn't use the same number? Flick punched in three–five–seven and pressed enter. She pulled on the door, but it wouldn't open. She tried one–two–three, zero–zero–zero and a few other combinations but nothing happened. She could be there for ever. She didn't even know how many digits were required.

She gave up, and hung the picture back up again. Then she walked back around the desk and sat down, turning her attention to the laptop. The screen lit up as she wiggled the mouse. There were some emails open, but what immediately grabbed Flick's attention was a program showing CCTV feeds from all over Linth. She used the mouse to maximize the images. There were dozens of them, perhaps hundreds. She scrolled through them. There were several angles of the town square, shots of street after street. She watched the tourists idly wandering about, completely unaware they were being spied on. There were even plenty of images from inside shops, and as Flick kept clicking, she found feeds from inside the flats above the shops.

By navigating a menu, Flick discovered that the feeds were grouped into areas. One area immediately stood out: the De Haas Hotel. She clicked on a folder and dozens of images filled her screen. She scrolled through these, and sure enough, there was a feed showing the inside of the Team Fox base. She maximized the image and stared at the chairs and the armchairs by the fake fire. De Haas could easily see what they were up to.

She closed the window and opened up De Haas's emails. The most recent had the subject: *The Bell System*.

Flick couldn't believe her luck. She opened it up excitedly and began to read.

To: thegreatfox@gmail.com
From: ursula@aol.com
Subject: The Bell System
Dear Fox,

There are a lot of rumours flying around about the Bell System – what it is and what it can be used for. So I thought I'd ask you direct. As the outgoing chancellor of the Global Order, I'm sure I don't need to remind you that I have the right to know the method behind any trick; however, I'm not going to ask because I understand how controversial this trick has become, and appreciate your concerns over its possible misuse. But I do want you to tell me what you can while keeping its secrets safe. We've all heard stories, but what I want to know are the facts.

All the best,

Ursula

To: ursula@aol.com

From: thegreatfox@gmail.com

Subject: Re: The Bell System

Dear Ursula,

I'm sorry that this trick came to light on your watch. It is incredibly dangerous so I'm glad you aren't asking for the method, because the fewer people who know how the Bell System works, the better. Samuel Lions has gone to make sure it is safe – we are both worried about it being used for the wrong purposes.

So, what can I tell you? In the 1960s there was a magician who went by the name of Echo. He performed a mentalism act mixed with some pseudo-science, but also some genuine science and psychology. He managed to catch the eye of the UK government, who were interested in using his powers for military research. This was the height of the Cold War and there were all sorts of experiments going on. They funded him to develop his skills to see if they could be used to control the population or defeat an invading Soviet army. Thus, the Porth Brea Project was born. The UK government built a research centre deep underground in a disused tin mine in Cornwall, and he went to work.

Many people claimed Echo was a fraud, and that the only magic trick he performed was to disappear with millions of taxpayers' money. But there are also plenty of rumours about what Echo did achieve. The Bell System is one of many stories to come out of the Porth Brea Project.

It is a device that Lions rebuilt from notes and parts he found inside Porth Brea, and these had been based on ideas that go back to the end of the Second World War. There were a lot of insane experiments conducted by the Nazis in the final days of their regime. The Bell, or Die Glocke as they called it, was one of them. It seems as if Echo found out how to build it, and so it became part of his research. The possible uses in a magic trick are obvious, and this was why Lions took an interest in it in the first place. If you can influence which card a person chooses or persuade them to make certain choices, the opportunities in a magic show are endless. Imagine being able to genuinely read an audience member's mind or control the choices they make.

Then there are the other uses. A person wielding the Bell System would become terrifyingly powerful. Lions and I think there are members of the Global Order who want to use it for something beyond magic. Maybe even sell its power to the highest bidder. This is why Samuel Lions and I will do everything in our power to keep it hidden.

Regards,

Fox

Flick sat back in the chair and stared numbly at the screen as it slowly dawned on her what was at stake.

16
The Watcher

A few miles outside Linth, Dominic Drake was sitting at a desk in his hotel room, watching a film clip for the third time. He was still smarting from the way the Fox had humiliated him last year during *The Great Fox Hunt*. This time he was ready, and things would be very different. He watched as the blinds were put into position, and then Charlie climbed the steps to the platform and his shadow was seen walking into the wall.

The trick itself was pretty easy to work out. Any time you needed to show a shadow doing something, the person clearly wasn't doing anything of the sort. Drake had seen similar tricks performed before. David Copperfield himself had walked through the Great Wall of China. Drake knew what had really happened.

The trick had started as soon as the blinds were lowered. Someone of a similar height to Charlie was hidden in the floor of the platform. As soon as the blinds were down, that person got out of his secret hiding place and crouched down, where his shadow wouldn't be seen. Charlie climbed the stairs and ducked inside the blinds. He then stayed by the entrance to the cube and his shadow double stepped forward into the light. Viewers would now assume they could see Charlie's shadow, but in reality they were watching his double.

Meanwhile, Charlie was climbing down through a secret opening into the stairs. The stairs were then wheeled away with Charlie inside, and the shadow double pretended to pass into the wall. This effect was achieved by the angle of the light. The double moved his shadow towards the wall, making it look like he was walking into it. In reality, he passed into an area that created no shadow and then climbed back through the secret hatch into the floor of the platform. The blinds were then dropped revealing the platform to be empty.

Charlie was now inside the steps. These were wheeled out of the castle gates and around to the outside of the wall, before being attached to the second platform in preparation for his reappearance. At this point Charlie climbed out of the steps and crawled along the platform floor to the wall, being careful not to create a shadow. He then stood up with his back against the wall, still making sure he didn't create a shadow. Finally, he moved forward into the spotlight and made it look like he was emerging out of the wall. The blinds were then raised, and Charlie was shown to be on the platform.

So far, so easy.

But what Drake found interesting was why Flick and Charlie had chosen to perform the trick at this particular location. Inside the castle walls, near the tower. And where was Flick? He had a strong suspicion that if she didn't feature in the trick then she was up to something, and he was very determined to find out what.

17
The Approach

Flick made her way out of Lukas De Haas's office and all the way down the stairs without being discovered. When she got to the bottom, she opened the green door a crack. The trick had finished, and the crew were packing up. The courtyard was a bustling melee of people and boxes – perfect to disguise her escape. She slowly opened the door and slipped out. She was still dressed like one of the crew so no one paid her any attention as she walked as fast as she could across the courtyard, out of the castle, and down the hill towards the hotel.

She needed to process the information she had read about Die Glocke. She had always assumed that her father had invented the Bell System, but it turned out that wasn't true. Another lie. Why hide the truth from her?

She trudged on down the steep zigzag road. Looking out across Linth, she could see the sun falling in the sky, turning the horizon fire red and dusting the underside of the clouds with pinks and purples, but even this beauty only signalled to Flick that time was marching on, another day was ending, and her chances of finding her dad were fading with the receding light.

Her thoughts churned.

Was it possible that the Fox had told Ursula the truth? Might her father have both discovered the Bell System and also reinvented it, in the sense that he found Echo's original parts and rebuilt it? The email said he had constructed it from notes and parts he had discovered in Porth Brea – so you could say he *had* reinvented it. And there was the fact that the Fox and her father were indeed apparently working together, as a team, keeping the Bell System hidden. That wasn't a lie. Her dad trusted the Fox, or at least tolerated him. Maybe he had no choice, and the Fox was the only one who would help him, or perhaps they really were friends. If that was the case, in order to help her dad, did she need to trust the Fox too?

Flick frowned as she arrived at the end of the zigzag road and made her way into town. She hadn't a clue what to do. After all this, she couldn't believe she was no further forward in understanding what was really going on.

The dying light was hitting the roofs and turning them gold, spotlighting sections of the cobbled streets and throwing long shadows. Some areas that were full of bars and cafes were coming to life, so Flick sought out a quieter street in the cool of the evening. She needed to think. Walking along with her head bowed, she tried to break the problem down into facts she knew for certain. If she didn't win the competition, she would be sent home, and how would that help her find her dad? Maybe trusting the Fox was her only option.

"Hello, Flick." Winston suddenly appeared beside her.

She jumped. Where had he come from? Had he been waiting in a dark doorway? She hadn't been paying attention to her surroundings.

He smiled at her. "So, do you want to know where your dad is?"

Flick ignored him and kept walking.

"Do you want to know?" he persisted.

Flick kept her eyes in front. One foot in front of the other.

"I was telling the truth when I said the Fox wants us to work together," he said.

Flick shook her head. "Why would the Fox want that?"

"There's a lot more going on here than this stupid competition. No one really cares about that. We're all here for the Bell System, and only by working together can we keep it safe."

Flick said nothing.

"Come on!" he exclaimed, throwing his arms wide. "We've found him. He's not here but we know where he is. And we can tell you. We can help him but we need to work together."

Flick stopped and looked at him. "He's not in Linth any more?"

"Nope."

Flick felt dizzy. "If I do work with you," she asked quietly, "will I be able to leave here straight away and go and see him?"

Winston hesitated. "Well, there are some things we need to do first."

"I just want to see my dad."

"What we've got to do here will help him, I promise."

Flick turned and continued walking down the hill again.

"OK, fine." He caught up with her. "We'll tell you where he is, once we've done what we have to do. Your dad would want us to do it, believe me. The Fox himself would have come and explained all of this to you but it's hard for us to sneak into Linth undetected – none of us are supposed to be here, remember, and the Fox is hardly inconspicuous."

Flick kept walking.

"So, do we have a deal?"

She said nothing.

He shrugged. "You're not saying no, so I'll take that as a yes. I'll be in contact," he said and wheeled away.

Flick stopped and watched him walk back up the hill towards the castle. When he had disappeared around the corner she turned and headed back to the hotel, more confused than ever.

18
The Consequences

Charlie sat alone in the Team Fox base wishing Flick would come and help him. The clock was ticking, and they were due back in the hot seats in a few hours' time to give the solution to Saanvi's trick. He climbed into the Fox pod and put on the VR goggles and gloves. Flick was the one who usually did this. Over the past six months, she had become an expert at navigating the database and could find tricks and solutions in seconds. But she had vanished, and time wasn't going to wait for her to turn up. Charlie would just have to get on with it.

He started to search through the database at random, looking for anything that resembled Saanvi's trick. He didn't know where to start. He cursed Flick's stubbornness. Why wouldn't she listen? They weren't going to win this competition unless they worked together. Sighing, he scrolled through trick after trick. The first few he looked at were completely different, but eventually he stumbled on one that was similar, and from there he finally found more. He clicked the buttons and watched virtual performance after virtual performance until his eyes were gritty and his mind was too tired to think.

But none of the tricks were quite right.

Still stumped, he removed his goggles. His back ached where he'd been hunched over concentrating for so long, and it was dark now. He yawned and then started to walk towards the door to put the light on and stretch his legs.

Hello, Charlie.

The voice was so deep the light fitting above the table rattled.

Do you trust the Fox?

Charlie stood very still.

I didn't think so. You're too smart for that. You're clever enough to know when you're being played.

He could hear the sound of breathing. It echoed around the room.

But I don't think you've worked out what he really wants. You know he's not interested in helping to find Flick's father. They were never really friends. And you know he's after something, but you don't know what.

Charlie looked around trying to work out where the voice was coming from.

Shall I tell you?

Charlie waited.

He's after something in the vault. Not the diamonds. Something far more valuable. In one of the deposit boxes is a painting that's been there since the Second World War. The painting is very valuable, but he's not interested in it for its monetary value. On the back of it are some plans – an early prototype of Die Glocke. Do you know what Die Glocke means? It's German for the Bell. The Fox wants those plans because, just like everyone else, he wants to use the power of the Bell System.

Charlie edged towards the door.

And you must be wondering where Flick is. She's with Synergy.

"Why would she be..." Charlie started but his voice croaked. He tried again. "She wouldn't..."

Oh yes, she would. You can't trust her. She doesn't care about you. All she really cares about is finding her dad and she'll happily betray you to do that.

Charlie swallowed.

And what about what you want? The Bell System could help your brother. He needs deep brain stimulation and that is exactly what the Bell System does. It gets right into the mind. Everyone wants it, Charlie, because everyone needs it, and they'll all trample over you to get to it. You need to look out for yourself.

The breathing stopped abruptly and was replaced by another sound coming from the door.

Charlie spun round and was relieved to see it was Flick swiping her key card.

"What are you doing standing here in the dark?" she asked, stepping through the door.

"What am I doing? What have *you* been doing, more like?"

"Oh, don't worry about that," Flick muttered, turning the light on.

Charlie shielded his eyes from the sudden bright glare. "Well, that's not very reassuring, is it? Have you been trying to work out Saanvi's trick?"

"No."

"Well, why not? How come I'm doing all the work here?" hissed Charlie angrily.

"I'm just about to start on that," Flick responded. "But listen, something weird just happened. I—"

"You promised to think about Saanvi's trick!" Charlie cried. "You keep going on about how the Fox has lied to us, but you just broke a promise. It's just as well one of us has been thinking about it or we'd soon be out of the competition and how would that help anyone? I thought we were a team, but it turns out you're just out for yourself. You do what you want and won't listen to me. In fact, it wouldn't surprise me if you were actually working for Drake. You certainly aren't trying to help the Fox win. And if we aren't a team, I don't know why I should wait around for you. You wouldn't wait for me, that's for sure."

With that Charlie stormed out, leaving Flick open-mouthed in shock.

19
The Trail

It was dinner time, but Flick didn't want to go to the dining room and risk bumping into Charlie. She wasn't remotely hungry anyway. They were supposed to be at the castle in a couple of hours to give their solution to Saanvi's trick, but she didn't want to think about that. She just wanted to spend some time in her room alone.

She was angry with Charlie for not understanding. He was just like everyone else – not interested in finding her dad. Well, if Charlie wasn't going to help her, she would have to do it all by herself – the way it had always been.

She switched on the bedside lamp and turned the main light off in an attempt to make her room feel more relaxing. Maybe it would do her good just to crawl into bed for a bit and have a nap.

She rang reception and asked them to give her a wake-up call in an hour. That would leave her just enough time to walk up to the castle. If Charlie was going to talk to her like that, then he could work out the solution to Saanvi's stupid trick on his own.

She sat on the edge of the bed and took off her prosthetic, slowly unclipping it and gently pulling the silicone cup away. She rolled down the socks cushioning her limb and inspected the damage from bumping down the castle stairs too fast. The end was raw. She gently massaged it, and closed her eyes. It felt good to let her limb breathe. She tried to relax but could feel the anguish from her argument with Charlie rising up from her stomach. She hadn't wanted to fall out with him, but he had acted like a prize idiot. She had to put her dad first. It was the right thing to do and always would be.

She hopped into the en suite, washed, changed into her pyjamas and then climbed into bed, turning off the bedside light. She lay there in the dark, hoping she could stop her mind working. But she couldn't help going over and over what she had discovered. Winston had said her dad had left Linth – was that true? And if it was, maybe Charlie was right – could it be that he didn't want to be found?

Eventually she slept, but her dreams were vivid and terrifying. A huge crack in the earth opened and she crawled to the edge to peer into the deep fissure. Below her she could see Charlie hanging on to a ledge, trying not to fall into the pit below. She reached out for him, and he grabbed her hand. But then she spotted her father on another ledge not far away, reaching out for her too. The ground was shaking as if in an earthquake, and both Charlie and her father were about to fall. She could only save one.

She woke up panting, drenched in sweat. The phone was ringing.

She sat up and answered the phone, thanking the receptionist, and then tried to shake the nightmare out of her head. After a few minutes, her breathing returned to normal and she swung her leg over the edge of the bed. Her prosthetic was propped up against the bedside table, so she grabbed it and took a liner out of the drawer. This had a pin on the end which she turned inside out to expose the silicone cup at the bottom. She placed this against her sore limb and rolled the liner up her leg, being careful to avoid any air bubbles. Then she took the two socks which she needed to pad her leg and rolled them over her limb and up to her thigh before sliding her limb into the prosthetic. Finally, she pushed herself up from the bed and stood, putting her full weight down until she heard the pin click into place.

She pulled on her shorts, got dressed and walked over to the window. A small slither of moon shone through the patchy clouds, casting its pale light on the rooftops of Linth. She tried to calm herself down, breathing in deeply and watching the clouds drift across the dark sky.

When she felt a bit calmer, she walked to the door and opened it. She was about to step out onto the landing when she spotted Harry and Ruby tiptoeing towards the stairs. Where were they off to? She pulled the door nearly shut and peeked through the gap. Watching them pass by, she waited for them to reach the top of the stairs before she started to follow them at a safe distance.

She made her way down and across the foyer and out into the night. Harry and Ruby were heading down the hill towards the harbour.

Flick froze as she spotted someone step out of the shadows and greet them. A man with a silver cane. Drake. What was he doing here? He was *also* breaking the rules of the competition.

She watched as they talked for a bit before Drake headed down the hill and Harry and Ruby turned back towards the hotel. Flick quickly dived into a shop doorway and watched Harry and Ruby go past. She only had a few seconds to decide what to do. By now she *should* be walking fast up the hill to the castle to meet Charlie and give Christina their solution to Saanvi's trick. but it felt like something more important was at stake here. What was Drake up to?

She made a quick decision and started to follow Drake as fast as her leg would allow. The magician was definitely heading towards the harbour, but luckily he didn't seem to be in any hurry as he ambled his way along the deserted streets and she soon caught him up. He looked like a man out for a stroll or a spot of window shopping, except it was dark and all the shops were shut. He was going so slowly she soon needed to slow down, which was a relief to her limb.

As he reached the harbour Drake turned left and followed the road that ran along the water's edge. There were lots of cafes, restaurants and taverns along this stretch. Most of these were closed, but every now and then bright light spilt out across the pavement and Flick could make out the raucous sounds of music and laughter coming from within as people enjoyed themselves.

Drake kept going.

Flick tucked in tight to the left hand-side of the road, close to the cafes and taverns. That way, if Drake looked round, she would be in the shadows, and if he did spot her, he might think she was just someone spilling out from a pub.

But he didn't turn round once.

Eventually he paused outside an open tavern. Flick hung back until he entered, and then she slipped from the shadows and examined the building. A large wooden sign hanging outside read *Altes Haus*. The front of the pub was a criss-cross of wooden beams and white plaster. It was only one storey high, and had a low tiled roof which sagged in the middle.

Flick peered in through the open door. The space inside was packed with rowdy drinkers. Drake had already vanished. There was no way she could follow him; she would stand out a mile and probably be asked to leave, which would definitely blow her cover. She stepped away from the door and tried to peek through one of the narrow windows, but she couldn't see any sign of Drake, so she moved along, trying all of them in turn.

No luck.

At the end of the building was a narrow alley, which she edged into. It was very dark, so she waited for her eyes to adjust. The alley ran alongside the pub and she could see light spilling out from another window further down. She crept towards the window. She had to stand on tiptoe to see in, and even then, she could only make out a couple of heads. Not much use. But then a new head appeared from the right. This one looked about the correct height and had the same grey hair as Drake. He was threading his way between happy punters and heading to the left. Towards the back of the pub.

Flick looked to her left. In the gloom, she could just make out a low door. She crept over and pushed it gently.

It opened.

It was pitch-black inside. She felt around and found a light switch. She listened in the dark for a few seconds, and when she was sure no one was there she flicked it on. Inside the door were some steps that disappeared under the pub. Perhaps down to a cellar, she guessed. Maybe this was where they brought the beer barrels. The steps were steep but there was a rail on the right. She looked at the dizzy gradient and hesitated. To be on the safe side, Flick went down backwards.

As she descended, she really hoped the cellar was empty –
backwards wasn't the ideal way to face an attacker.

When she eventually arrived at the bottom she turned
round and discovered the cellar was full of beer barrels with
pipes running upwards through the ceiling. She could hear
the noisy punters upstairs, the sounds of scraping chairs and
muffled chatter filtering through the floorboards. She looked
up as she walked along, trying to work out her bearings.
Where was the room Drake was in? She figured the pipes
must lead to the bar, so she veered to the left, in the direction
Drake's head had been travelling. If it *had* been his head.

At the end of the cellar was a dark tunnel that sloped
upwards. She got on her hands and knees and crawled up
the incline. She could see light coming from above and edged
forward. She found herself in a narrow wedge where the ramp
met the ceiling, and here she discovered a hatch. Maybe this
was where they rolled the barrels down into the cellar. At the
edge of the hatch was a gap. Flick peered through the crack.

She was looking into a back room. And right there in front
of her was Dominic Drake.

20
The Global Order

Flick couldn't see much through the crack at the edge of the hatch, so she tilted her head and tried to find a better angle. She could see Drake sitting at a table with several other people, but she couldn't see any of their faces.

"And not just missing out," Drake was saying. "We have a duty to use it. For the future of the Global Order."

"How would it help us?" asked a thin and reedy voice.

"The Global Order is struggling financially," Drake replied impatiently. "We have a lot of debt. The Bell System is commercial gold dust. Think of its power if used in advertising – you could compel people to buy your products. Imagine the money that could be made."

"But that would be illegal," pointed out another voice, this one deep and gruff.

"Oh, come on! Someone would be prepared to use it and be happy to pay a fortune for the privilege."

"Does it work?" asked the thin and reedy voice.

"Obviously we haven't been able to get our hands on Lions' machine yet. However, we do have an early prototype. It's not perfect – it's a work in progress – but it's a start."

"Really? And how exactly have you managed that?" asked the voice.

"De Haas found plans that had been secretly stored in his bank vault since the Second World War and has used them to build an early version of what we think Samuel Lions has. This is why the competition is being held in Linth. I persuaded Ursula to hold it here so that I could demonstrate the prototype to you. I want you to see it in action."

Flick stifled a gasp.

"Does Ursula know about the prototype?" asked the gruff voice.

"No. We've tried to keep it a secret. That's why I'm only telling you about it now."

"What about the Fox? Does he know there's a prototype?" asked a third voice that belonged to a woman.

"I think he's worked it out. He certainly suspects there are some plans in the vault. He's going to make his team perform his final trick there and I imagine that's because he wants to try and find them."

"But if Lions already has his complete working Bell

System, why is the Fox interested in the prototype?" asked the thin voice.

"It seems Lions has disappeared in order to make sure the Bell System is safe, and I believe that includes keeping it away from the Fox. I think the Fox is just as interested in exploiting the power of the Bell System as we are."

"But I thought they were friends?" the thin voice responded.

"They were. Until recently. But my sources tell me they've fallen out."

Flick felt her stomach knot. She had almost convinced herself that she needed to give the Fox the benefit of the doubt. Now it seemed as if she had been right about him all along.

"How do we stop the Fox?" asked the gruff voice.

"Leave that to me. His snooping around in the vault will not end well. De Haas will make sure of that."

"Suppose we manage to perfect the prototype. How would we find a company willing to use it?" wondered the woman.

"I've already got several lined up who are interested."

"What would they be willing to pay?" asked the thin voice.

"We're talking tens of millions."

There was silence for a beat as the sheer scale of this number sank in.

"So I need your help to win this competition," said Drake. "If I win, the future of the Global Order will be lucrative for all of us."

"I'm not so sure," muttered the gruff voice.

"Listen," said Drake. "I'm so confident in the money we can make I'm prepared to pay for your help up front."

There was a pause.

"We're listening," said the woman softly.

"The plans are not the only valuable thing in that vault. There are several deposit boxes which haven't been opened since the Second World War. In those boxes certain high-ranking Nazi officers deposited millions in stolen artwork and treasures. I can get my hands on some of these and share them with you … *if* you help me win."

"And how are you going to get them out of the bank?" asked the woman doubtfully.

"Like I said, the Fox's apprentices are going to perform their final trick in the vault. We can blame them for the missing painting and anything else we decide to remove. I have it all worked out."

"Very well. And you can arrange a demonstration of the prototype's power?" asked the thin voice.

"Make sure you are present for the closing ceremony, when they show the finished tricks and announce the winner, and when the moment comes, remember to wear the goggles and ear protectors," said Drake. "I guarantee that you will like what you see."

"I think we have a deal," said the woman.

"Agreed," said the gruff voice.

"Then I wish you all a good evening," said Drake.

There was the sound of chairs scraping on the floor. Flick edged further forward to try to catch a glimpse of the others as they were leaving. She pushed her eye hard up against the hatch, straining to see.

And then the hatch gave way.

With a loud creak, Flick tumbled through the opening onto the floor.

Drake spun round. "Hello." He smiled nastily, looking down at Flick. "Nice of you to join us, Felicity."

Flick frantically pulled herself up and just managed to slip back inside the opening as he lunged towards her. She pulled the hatch shut and crawled as fast as she could back down the tunnel.

Drake lifted the hatch and called after her. "Thought you could spy on me?" he laughed, and then Flick heard him slamming the hatch shut.

She made her way back across the cellar as fast as she could and started to climb the stairs. She was halfway up when the door above her flew open.

Drake looked down at her and sneered. "Unfortunately for you, this door locks from the outside."

And then he slammed that shut too.

Flick heard the bolt slide across.

She reached the top of the stairs, but he was right – there wasn't even a handle on the inside. She pushed and pushed but the door wouldn't budge. She crouched down and tried to squeeze her fingers underneath the bottom edge to move it, but it was stuck fast. She hobbled back down the stairs and across the cellar and crawled her way up the slope to the hatch, but that wouldn't open either.

She felt the panic rise inside her. If she couldn't get out, it would be the end of the competition. Charlie wouldn't be allowed to carry on alone so the Fox would lose, and Drake would get his hands on the workings of the Bell System. She didn't trust the Fox, but the thought of Drake with all that power was truly terrifying. If he won, all the sacrifices her father had made would be for nothing, and it would all be her fault.

She pushed at the hatch again, but it didn't move. She dug her heels in and gave it a really big heave, but it still didn't budge and she just slowly slid back down to the bottom of the tunnel.

When would someone come and find her? Maybe someone would check the cellar before the pub closed for the night. But possibly not. She might have to wait until the morning. She crawled out of the tunnel, leant back against the wall and rested her head against the cold stone.

It was going to be a long night.

21
The Team

Charlie walked onto the stage in the castle's great hall on his own. He felt sick. Flick was nowhere to be found and it was time to give their solution. He shouldn't have got so angry with her. He'd clearly upset her and now they were in big trouble.

A large screen had been erected at one end of the stage and there was a little platform with two chairs for them to sit on at the other. Charlie would only be needing one. He watched the screen anxiously while they played the Studio Three Crew's trick again. There was a camera trained on his face so that his reactions would be captured for the show.

He tried to look like he was in control, while inside his mind continued to race.

When the trick had finished, Christina walked onto the stage and stood in front of the screen while the usual three make-up artists fussed about her. Finally, when everyone was happy, they cued her in.

"Charlie, welcome back to the hot seats. We're sorry your fellow apprentice isn't with you. You say Flick has been taken ill?"

Charlie clenched his jaw and nodded.

"Poor girl," Christina continued. Then she looked directly down the lens so that the audience could appreciate the depth of her concern and said, "Let's all hope she feels better soon."

She paused for the perfect amount of time and then looked at Charlie, saying, "Now, your team are the last up, so I can tell you that Team Drake worked out Synergy's trick in six minutes and forty-three seconds. Synergy worked out your trick in one minute and thirty-eight seconds, and the Studio Three Crew failed to work out how Team Drake performed their trick, meaning Team Drake automatically go through and the Studio Three Crew are definitely heading home. So, you need to work out how the Studio Three Crew performed this trick in less than one minute and thirty-eight seconds, or I'm afraid Team Fox will also be going home."

Charlie gulped.

Christina paused and smiled at him but it was purely for the cameras. While her mouth beamed her eyes remained cold and refused to join in.

"So, can you work out in less than one minute and thirty-eight seconds how Saanvi did her trick? Your time starts ... NOW!"

"Erm," said Charlie hurriedly. "Right. Well, she took a pack of cards and gave it to the woman to cut. There was nothing funny about the way that was done. And then the boy counted the cards, so that wasn't forced. He could have changed his mind. In fact, he did change his mind! So the trick wasn't in the cut or the count." He tried to think logically. "When the woman put the card back in her half of the deck, it wasn't shuffled. So Saanvi might have been able to force where it went back in..."

He really wished Flick were there.

"What I mean is, Saanvi got her to put the card back in the deck and it wasn't shuffled," Charlie continued. "That's important. So, at that point, she might have known where the card was. It was cut at the start and split into two portions. I think that's the method."

He gave a quick smile. He was on a roll now. "Before the trick started, Saanvi removed all the eights and nines from the deck. Then she placed these at the top with another card in between each of them. So, when she spreads out the cards the pack looks shuffled, but it isn't. The woman then cuts the top off the deck and gives it to the man. Those eights and nines are still every other card in that portion. She then chooses a card from her half of the deck. Totally free selection. Saanvi then takes her half of the deck and cuts it, holding it open for the woman to slip her card back in. Saanvi must have counted off eight cards and then she makes sure the chosen card goes in at number nine. That's why there is no shuffle. The boy then counts out the cards. Saanvi made him do it slowly, so he doesn't go too far. He has to stop before the top sixteen cards are used up because that's where the eights and nines are. Every other card is either an eight or a nine in that section, so all Saanvi has to do is count and know if the boy stopped on an even or odd number. If it's odd they take the next card. If the card is an eight you deal out eight cards and it's the next one. If it's a nine it is the ninth card. That's how she did it!"

Charlie took a deep breath and looked at Christina, who held her finger to her ear. "We're just checking if that is the correct solution... And I can reveal that..." She paused for dramatic effect.

The thumping bass of a heartbeat started pounding from the speakers on the stage.

Charlie leant forward nervously in his seat.

"Congratulations!" cried Christina. "You worked it out in one minute and thirty seconds, so you are through to the final round. And this means we will sadly be saying goodbye to the Studio Three Crew and Synergy. That leaves Team Fox and Team Drake to go head to head in the final!"

22
The Doubt

Flick spent the night in the cellar. It was definitely a contender for the longest night of her life. It was cold and dark, and something that occasionally squeaked kept scuttling around in one corner. She slept in fits and starts, willing the time to pass. Eventually, in the morning, the barman opened the cellar door and turned on the light. Unsurprisingly he was shocked to find a girl sitting on the floor at the bottom of the steps, blinking tiredly at him. It didn't help that Flick didn't speak any German, but after a while, she managed to get him to phone the hotel. He wouldn't let Flick leave until an adult came to collect her, so she sat in the empty bar and ravenously worked her way through a selection of free crisps and soft drinks until her escort arrived.

Flick was surprised to see the Fox turn up.

"I insisted on coming to get you myself," the magician explained.

He thanked the barman in stilted German and then they stepped out into the sunshine. The irony was not lost on Flick that the barman thought it was unsafe for her to walk back to the hotel on her own, yet he was totally fine letting her leave with a man wearing a huge fox mask.

"You OK?" asked the Fox.

"I'm fine. Just a bit tired. Didn't exactly get much sleep."

"How on earth did you end up in there?"

Flick wondered how much she should tell him. The whole Global Order of Magic seemed to be corrupt. Was there anyone she could trust?

She took a deep breath. "I followed Drake. He locked me in the cellar."

"Drake was here?" the Fox said, sounding concerned.

"Yes."

"He's not supposed to be in town. None of the mentors are. They've only let me come back to find you. They wanted to send Gemma, but I insisted on coming myself because I was worried something had happened to you. Half the crew were out last night searching for you after Charlie finally raised the alarm when he realized you weren't back at the hotel. I've told them I'll take you to the Team Fox base. You'll be safe there, and then I'm under strict instructions to leave town again immediately."

The early morning streets were quiet as the two of them made their way along the harbour. They passed several fishing boats tied up and a selection of impressive motor yachts in a marina. The only noise was a seagull swooping overhead shouting loudly to his friends.

The Fox slowed so Flick could keep up. "What was Drake up to?"

"He met several people who I think were members of the Global Order."

"They're not supposed to be here either. What were they doing?"

Flick shrugged. "I felt it best not to come out of my hiding place and ask them."

The Fox looked at her.

She relented. "Drake told them about some plans he has for a prototype Bell System."

The Fox stopped in his tracks. "Are you sure?"

Flick looked at him and pointed to her face. "This isn't just tiredness."

"If that's true then..." He trailed off and started walking again.

Flick bumped along beside him. "There's more. Drake is planning on stealing a fortune in lost valuables from the vault. He says there are lots of treasures and artwork that were stolen by the Nazis and hidden in there during the Second World War. He was offering to give some of them to the Global Order council members if they agreed to help him."

"Help him do what?"

"Win the competition."

The Fox shook his head and stomped on in silence.

"Which, apart from being a disaster," Flick said, "leaves me with some big questions. In particular, how can there be earlier plans for a prototype if the Bell System was invented by my dad?"

"It's complicated," said the Fox.

"Try me." Flick him closely. She thought she knew the answer from the emails she had read in the tower, but would the Fox be honest with her?

The Fox walked on in silence.

Flick stopped. "I'm not doing this any more. I can't trust anything you say. My dad didn't invent the Bell System, did he? And where is he? Do you even know? Do you really need me for this competition, or are you just using me as some sort of bargaining chip to get to him?"

"No," he protested. "Of course not. OK, I'll try to explain. Your dad rediscovered the Bell System, if you like, and by the time he'd finished experimenting he realized he had something truly terrifying on his hands. He had heard the stories of a magician called Echo. Echo was part of a secret government project during the Cold War to build the Bell System in a disused mine in Cornwall. A couple of years ago your dad secretly visited the mine and explored the miles of tunnels, and eventually he found the Bell. Once he rebuilt it and I realized what the Bell System was capable of, we vowed to stop anyone else getting their hands on it, whatever the cost. But there is a set of plans out there for an earlier version built at the end of the Second World War. Which is a disaster. If Drake persuades the Global Order members to help him win..."

"And what about the answers to all my other questions?"

"It's complicated. The only thing I can say is that I'm doing everything I can to work with your father to keep the Bell System out of the hands of Drake and others who would abuse it. We're on the same side, Flick, believe me."

"And what does the Bell System really do? You've never actually told me."

The Fox checked they were alone before moving closer to Flick and lowering his voice to a whisper. "It uses very bright lights and extremely loud sounds to overload the brain and put a person into an altered mental state. It might erase certain memories or put them into a trance. It is possible it can influence their thinking and force them to follow your commands. Until it is used on someone, and the results are recorded, we can't say for sure. But we do know for certain that it is incredibly powerful. Even if only half our suspicions about its capabilities are true, that would still make it very dangerous. Imagine if it was used in a political campaign.

People would unknowingly be forced to vote for a particular candidate. Or what if it could erase someone's memory entirely? That is why your father and I will do everything in our power to keep it hidden."

"And where *is* my dad? You do know, don't you? Why won't you just tell me?"

The Fox shook his head. "Right now, I don't know where he is."

Flick glared at him.

They trudged on in silence for a beat until Flick eventually asked, "And how come you didn't know about these plans?"

Fox sighed. "I did. I thought De Haas could be trusted when I told him what I thought was in his vault. I persuaded Ursula to have the competition here so I could perform a trick which gave me an excuse to get into the bank, and then I was planning on removing the painting and destroying it so that those plans don't reach the wrong hands. But it seems as if De Haas betrayed me and got to the painting first."

"That's bad," said Flick.

"Yes, it is," agreed the Fox. "Come on. Let's get you somewhere I know you'll be safe."

They resumed walking up the hill, side by side. Flick scowled. She believed the Fox was telling the truth, or at least a version of it. But there was still so much that he hadn't told her; so many gaps. Then there was the fact that the whole Global Order seemed to be after the Bell System. Everyone seemed to want to get their hands on it and that meant they were all after her dad. She didn't like to think about what they would do to him when they found him.

They crossed the square outside the hotel which was completely empty. There weren't even any guests enjoying an early morning coffee yet. The door to the hotel was open though, and a waiter had just come through it to start opening out the umbrellas and setting out the chairs. The Fox ducked through the door and Flick followed. They crossed the deserted reception and passed the stairs to the door that led into the car park. Fox opened this and then strode towards their team base.

"Have you got your key card?" he asked.

Flick reached into her pocket and removed it, holding it up.

"Good. I've got to go," said the Fox. "If they find out I hung around for a minute too long we might get disqualified."

The Fox turned to go back across the car park towards the hotel, but then paused and faced Flick. "We'll talk again. I promise I'll tell you more when I can."

Flick nodded but said nothing. She watched as the Fox walked across the car park and disappeared into the hotel. When he was out of sight, she turned towards the base, and taking her key the door swished open. She slipped inside and turned on the lights. As the doors slid shut, she took in a deep breath.

"So glad you could join me," said a voice from an armchair by the fire.

Flick jumped as Lukas stood up.

He was wearing dark green silk trousers and a matching waistcoat over a billowing white shirt. Nero sat on the floor at his feet and regarded Flick with cold eyes.

Flick stepped away from the door and away from Lukas, towards the table and chairs.

Nero bared his teeth and growled.

"Oh, ignore him," said De Haas. "He's in a right grump today. Anyway, young lady. There's something I want to show you."

The doors swished open and in walked Dominic Drake, carrying a large wooden box. He stood in the doorway and smiled.

"Hello again," he said.

Flick edged towards one of the wooden chairs around the table, placing a hand on it. She might be able to use it as a weapon.

Drake stepped forwards and placed the wooden box in the middle of the room, and Lukas walked over and opened it, lifting out a large black object suspended inside a metal frame. He placed it carefully on the floor.

"You know Dominic, don't you?" Lukas asked without looking up. "And I expect you can probably guess what this is."

Flick stared at it. It was bell-shaped.

"It's only tiny compared with your father's version and nowhere near as powerful. But we'd like you to help us out with it."

Flick said nothing.

Drake didn't take his eyes off Flick. "No one alive has ever seen the full effects of Die Glocke. We're about to make history," he said quietly.

De Haas reached into the box again and this time he pulled out a large remote control. The back was a mess of wires and on the front was a complex array of dials and buttons. He pressed a couple of buttons and turned one of the dials.

"We're going to switch it on in a minute and then we're going to ask you to tell us everything about the trick you're performing for the final round. We want to know all the Fox's plans. And when we're done with that, we're going to ask you where your dad is," he said.

"I – I don't know where he is," tried Flick.

"We'll see," responded Drake.

De Haas took a bag out of the box and pulled out two pairs of black goggles and some ear defenders. He handed a set to Drake and they both put them on. De Haas reached down and flicked a final switch on his remote control and then he retreated from the Bell, standing next to Drake with their backs to the door.

The Bell started to spin.

Flick watched as it spun faster and faster, making a whistling noise at first and then a deeper and deeper sound. Soon it started to roar. Flick backed away until she was touching the wall. The Bell spun faster still, sparks flying out. These turned to flashes that grew in size until lightning arced outwards, hitting the furniture and the ceiling. Flick couldn't move; she was pinned against the wall. The flashes were so bright it was hard to see. She shut her eyes and turned her head away.

And then the Bell started to whine, its tone getting higher and higher.

Flick clamped her hands over her ears, but the sound filled her mind – a high-pitched screech that was so loud it consumed her. Her eyes were still tightly shut, and she had no desire to open them.

And then...

Perfect silence.

Flick took her hands away from her ears and slowly opened her eyes.

All she could see was white.

A featureless, colourless plane stretched in all directions. It was like looking into infinity. The floor seemed solid, and she tried taking a few steps. It was the same colour as the ceiling and everything all around her. Her eyes couldn't judge distances. The whiteness continued for ever.

Flick started to panic. She could feel it rising and growing inside her.

She opened her mouth and screamed.

PART THREE

Answers

In which you realize you've been
looking in the wrong direction.
You thought you were one step ahead
of the magician only to discover you
were a long, long way behind.

23
The Police

Victor Odermatt sat at his desk and rubbed his face. He was tired. He loved his job, he really did. He was methodical and persistent, well organized and had a nose for the truth. Some of his superior officers in the past had even described him as brilliant, and during his long career, there had been several standout investigations that suggested that was so. But what he disliked, what made him feel like giving it all up and walking away, was politics. He had risen through the ranks to chief of police for the district of Linth and it seemed as if each step up the ladder took him further from the job he loved and forced him to spend more time compromising.

There was an example of this on his desk right now.

He sipped his camomile tea. It was hot and strong, just the way he liked it, but it failed to lift his mood. It didn't relax him like it was supposed to. Perhaps it was time for a little Mozart – would that do the trick? He kept a record player on his desk for moments such as these. He twisted round and pulled out a record sleeve from the shelf behind him. Symphony No. 41. A favourite. He placed the record on the turntable, gently lowered the needle and closed his eyes.

As he listened, his mind drifted to his police force with their limited resources. Currently they were dealing with twenty-four residential break-ins, sixteen thefts from vehicles, two assaults, one suspicious homicide and an investigation into drug trafficking. His force was busy. In fact, they were overstretched, but he couldn't say that, except in private. Victor reported to the mayor of Linth, Josef Fischer, a man who would not be happy if his police chief admitted there were not enough police officers. That would not be good for votes. It was important to public perception that the police were always in control. So politics meant Victor kept his mouth shut and tried to get the job done.

And then, to add insult to injury, the mayor dumped a magic trick on his desk.

A magic trick! Of all the things he needed to deal with.

Mayor Fischer considered Lukas De Haas to be a good friend, probably because the banker had made a very generous contribution to the mayor's last election campaign.

The two men were a prominent part of the Linth elite, where rich businessmen mixed with the men and women of power. No doubt they played golf together too; Victor didn't really care.

The fact was, De Haas had spoken to the mayor and demanded a meeting with his chief of police to discuss a television show being filmed in his bank, and that meant that on top of the very real crimes he had to deal with, Victor would now have to investigate a pretend robbery. A robbery where the owner of the bank had invited the thief and a camera crew into his vault, where the owner had agreed to be robbed, and where the thief had agreed to return the stolen property. What a waste of Victor's meagre resources, simply because De Haas and Mayor Fischer shared the same putting green.

Victor's secretary buzzed through the news that De Haas had arrived. Victor stopped his record player, sat up straighter in his chair and tried to compose himself. He needed to smile, nod and be nice, and not let his irritation show.

As De Haas entered the room, Victor stood and said politely, "Welcome, Mr De Haas. How nice to see you." He gestured for his guest to sit.

De Haas smiled widely at him and they shook hands. "Thank you so much for agreeing to see me. I appreciate you're a busy man."

Victor nodded. "You have no idea," he replied.

"Then I will get straight to the point. As I believe you already know, a TV show is shortly going to be filmed in my bank. The premise of the show is to make some very valuable diamonds disappear from my vault. The company which insures my bank is understandably a little nervous about letting this trick take place, and they are seeking certain assurances."

De Haas paused and looked at Victor to see if he was following. Victor sat impassively.

Lukas continued. "To get to the point, what they need to know is that there will be an officer assigned to this case."

Victor stared at him.

Lukas hurried to fill the silence. "Do you think that would be possible?"

"Mr De Haas. There *is* no case, therefore I cannot assign an officer to it. Isn't the whole point of this exercise that nothing is actually stolen?"

"Yes. That is correct."

"Then what exactly are you asking me to do?"

"My insurers want the reassurance of knowing that there will be a police presence at the event."

"Mr De Haas, you live in a very safe town. Switzerland has a reputation for being one of the safest countries in the world. It is thanks to the tremendous hard work and dedication of men and women like those found in my department that this is the case. But we are only so many. We cannot be everywhere."

"I understand this, Mr Odermatt, and may I take this opportunity to express how much I appreciate all that hard work and dedication. But I spoke to the mayor this morning, and he assured me this would not be a problem."

Victor frowned. "You will notice, Mr De Haas, that on the door you have just come through it says *Chief of Police*. Not *Mayor*. I decide what my officers do and do not do."

"I see," Lukas said, still smiling.

"If you are asking me whether I will investigate the crime should one occur in your bank vault, the answer is yes, I will. I might question the wisdom of inviting someone to try and steal something from you, but that is up to you. It is also up to you to appease your insurance company. If you choose to embark on such a risky course of action, I can understand why they would be concerned, but that is for you to sort out with them. Here we investigate crime, Mr De Haas. If no crime is committed, we do not investigate."

Lukas's smile finally vanished. "I was assured by Mayor Fischer that an officer would be assigned to this matter."

Victor sighed inwardly. He'd given it his best shot but the outcome was inevitable. "Since I deem this whole process to be a total waste of time for my highly trained officers, I will not be assigning anyone. However, since the mayor has made you a promise, this department must honour it. I will assign myself. Tell your insurance people the chief of police himself will be responsible. That should shut them up."

"And you will be on site for the night of the show?"

"Don't push your luck, Mr De Haas."

Lukas stood up to leave. "I appreciate your dedication and kindness, Mr Odermatt. Thank you."

With that he gave a little bow and left.

Victor returned to his camomile tea and took a long sip.

It had gone cold.

24
The Plan

Harry and Ruby climbed the stairs in the tower. When they got to the top, Harry knocked on the door.

"Come in," called Drake.

Lukas De Haas was sitting behind the large wooden desk and Drake was standing at his side, tapping his cane impatiently on the floor and gesturing to a couple of chairs in front of the desk.

"Good of you to join us," said De Haas. "Please take a seat."

Harry and Ruby sat down cautiously.

"We wanted to reassure you," said Drake smoothly. "Everything is under control."

"You shouldn't even be here, Mr Drake," pointed out Harry. "It's against the rules. What if you get caught?"

"Relax," said De Haas. "No one will know."

"He's worried about what Mummy will say," said Ruby.

"That's not true," Harry retorted crossly. "Why would you say that?"

"Just keep calm," said Drake. "The plans we have in place for the final trick are perfect."

"Except it involves cheating," said Harry.

"Look," said Drake. "All magic involves cheating. The trick does involve bending the rules, but that's how tricks work. The whole point of magic is to fool people. OK?"

Ruby nodded but Harry scowled.

"All you have to do is keep it together and we'll do the rest," said Drake. "You want to make your mother proud, don't you? Isn't that what you want?"

Harry shrugged. "I suppose so."

"Then how does winning this competition sound?" Drake asked.

Ruby nodded while Harry fidgeted.

"We now know exactly what the Fox and the one-legged girl are planning for their final trick," said De Haas. "We know all the details."

"How do you know?" asked Ruby curiously.

De Haas laughed. "She told us. They're going to fall right into our trap. After she performs the trick, she'll be removed from the competition, and that will leave us as the only team left. Just do as we say, and we'll win. It really is that simple."

25
The Pain

Flick opened her eyes and slowly took in her surroundings. She was standing in the Team Fox base by the table and chairs with her back pressed against the wall. She tried to move her head and winced at the splitting pain. It felt like someone had hit her with an axe. Running her hands over her forehead, she checked for any wounds or bumps but couldn't find any. Apparently there had been no axe. At least that was something.

The light coming from the chandelier caught her eye and caused more pain to shoot through her head. She turned away from the glare, yanked out a chair from under the table and collapsed onto it.

She paused for a moment, trying to make sense of what had happened before coming to a decision. She breathed slowly in and out before trying to stand again. Shakily, she made her way to the small toilet at the back of the base where she fumbled to get the door open.

The light pinged on inside and Flick shielded her eyes as she reached into a small corner cabinet where there was a first-aid kit. In the front pocket were painkillers, and she pushed one out of the blister pack and grabbed a glass on the basin, quickly filling it with water and washing it down. It made her feel sick as soon as she swallowed it. At least that took her mind off her head.

She examined her face in the mirror. It looked very pale but otherwise OK. What had happened to her? She could remember following Drake to the tavern and eavesdropping on his conversation. She could remember recounting this to the Fox. But after that, it was all a blank. How did she get back here?

She rubbed her head and tried to think.

She stared in the mirror at the wall behind her. The wall was white. Very white.

And then it hit her. De Haas and Drake with Die Glocke. What had they done to her? She remembered the bright flashing lights and the sound of Lukas's voice, but she couldn't recall what he'd said. Or what had happened afterwards.

Flick slowly staggered back to the armchairs by the fake fire, sat down and looked at her watch. She had an hour before lunch ended. Hopefully, that would be enough time for the painkillers to kick in, and for her to feel human again.

She lay back in the chair, closed her eyes and used all her energy to think through the pain. De Haas and Drake had Die Glocke, or some version of it. It wasn't as powerful as the Bell System, but the fact they possessed it had massive implications. Look what it had done to her. She was a wreck, with whole chunks of her memory missing. What power had they exercised over her? What had they made her tell them?

De Haas and Drake had to be stopped. At all costs. And that meant Flick had to help the Fox win the competition. Although she still didn't trust him, she was going to have to work with him. Her dad would have to wait.

She got up, rushed to the toilet and vomited in it. Twice. When she had finished and flushed, the sick feeling subsided. A wave of clarity washed over her and she could see more clearly. She knew what she had to do. It was time to go to work.

26
The Preparation

Flick slowly made her way to the dining room. She nearly lost her balance a couple of times in the corridor, and had to lean against the wall because she felt so woozy, but she eventually made it in one piece. She wondered how Charlie had got on with solving Saanvi's trick last night and felt a pang of guilt that she hadn't helped and that their last conversation together had not been … good. She hoped he'd worked it out or they were in big trouble. The dining room was nearly empty when she arrived, and the hotel staff were wiping down the tables and tidying the chairs. There wasn't much food left, so she chose a big portion of lasagne and sat down at a table on her own.

She thought through the positives. She was still alive. That was a plus. And that was pretty much it. Charlie had been right: finding her dad wasn't the top priority. Maybe her dad didn't even want to be found. She needed to concentrate on what was possible, the difference she could actually make, and not worry about what was beyond her control. That's what her dad would tell her, which was ironic because he *was* the thing that was beyond her control. It all meant concentrating on winning the competition.

De Haas and Drake had to be stopped.

She felt hungry now, which she took to be a good sign, and quickly munched her way through the large slabs of pasta and mince. When she had finished, she made her way into the ballroom. On the table were some new instructions from the Fox, tasks he wanted her to practise. Flick was determined, despite her pounding head, to give the trick her best shot.

The first task on the list was picking a lock. The Fox had found her an exact replica of the one she would need to pick on the deposit box at the bank – an old-style pin and tumbler.

The Fox had set the lock into a wooden drawer, and Flick's job was to pick the lock and open it. Sounded straightforward enough. To do this he had given her a tension wrench and a thin lock pick, standard tools of the trade. Flick had never used anything like them before: the L-shaped tension wrench was made of metal, about six centimetres long; the pick was a similar size but straight and thin. Despite her headache, Flick needed to learn fast and get this right because a vital part of the trick depended on it.

A pin and tumbler lock consists of a cylinder that can rotate within a housing. When locked, the cylinder is prevented from turning by several sets of pins. The pins are in pairs and the top pin of each set passes through the cylinder and into the housing, stopping it from moving. When the correct key is inserted, the grooves and ridges push the pins up so that they no longer stop the cylinder from rotating. When this happens, the cylinder can be turned by the key and the lock will open. Easy.

The first thing you need to do is place the pick into the upper part of the lock. This is pressed upwards so you can feel the individual pins with the tip. The next step is to find the hardest pin to push up. The goal is to push the pin high enough so that it is out of the cylinder. Then you need to repeat this process for the other pins until the lock opens.

Flick's first go took her sixteen minutes. On her second, she was able to do it in half the time. She had a third go and it took her about five minutes. But she knew the Fox wouldn't be satisfied. He wanted her to practise until she could do it in under two minutes. For this part of the trick to work, speed was crucial.

The Fox had also left some very detailed instructions about what to do when she opened the deposit box, and added *IMPORTANT!* in capitals next to them. The Fox had been planning for Flick to remove the painting from the deposit box so that it could be destroyed, permanently keeping the plans on it out of the wrong hands. But it seemed that De Haas had beaten them to it, and the Fox now expected that there would be no painting in the box to destroy. Instead, when Flick opened the box, she was to make absolutely sure the camera recorded the empty box before closing the door.

To give her a break from lock picking, the Fox's instructions also asked her to practise the diamond box switch again. Flick took off her hoodie, put on the special overalls over her shorts and T-shirt, and stood in front of the glass table with her back to it. With her left hand, she reached behind to the centre of the table and pulled the diamond box towards her. Then she removed the empty box from the hidden pouch on her back and placed it on the table next to the real one. She then picked up the one with the diamonds in it and slid it into her pouch.

All afternoon Flick worked without a break, practising each task so many times she lost count.

Whenever she became sick of switching the boxes, it was back to lock picking. By the end of the day, she could open the drawer in about a minute. Every time.

Utterly exhausted, Flick finally took her overalls off, put her hoodie back on, and went for dinner.

27
The Insurance

Victor Odermatt sat at his desk. He had moved on from camomile tea and was sipping black coffee. That should do the trick. The phone rang and he picked it up.

"Yes."

"Sir, I have a call for you from a Mr Landolt from Winterthur Insurance. He says it concerns a TV show at the De Haas Bank."

Victor sighed. "Very well. Put him through."

There was a click on the line.

"Mr Landolt, you are through to the chief of police for Linth. How may I help you?"

"Ah, Mr Odermatt. It is so nice to talk to you. You're a very busy man and hard to get hold of."

"I am indeed, so use your time wisely, Mr Landolt."

"Very well. I would like to confirm with you some of the details concerning the upcoming magic show at De Haas Bank."

Victor sipped his coffee and said, "Continue."

"Will you be on site when the trick takes place?"

"No. I will not."

"Ah, that is a shame. We were hoping to have a police presence at the bank on Friday evening for security reasons."

"I am the chief of police, Mr Landolt. I have more important things to attend to."

"Which is why we were a bit surprised that you had assigned yourself to oversee this matter. Would it not be more prudent to give it to one of your officers? Then they might have the time to be on hand for the event."

"My valuable officers are busy fighting real crime, Mr Landolt."

"Then perhaps you would like to reconsider being present yourself? It would be fabulous for you to be on television, would it not? You could be part of the great spectacle."

"Mr Landolt, I hate magic, I hate mindless television and I hate having my time wasted."

"Very well. Then do I have your word that you will at least watch the broadcast? From an insurance point of view, we need to make sure the assigned officer is aware of whatever happens."

Victor sighed heavily. "OK. Fine. I will do that."

"Good. I suggest you watch very closely, Mr Odermatt. Very closely indeed."

28
The Fountain

Flick arrived for dinner and spotted Charlie sitting at a table by himself. She walked over and plonked down her tray.

Charlie looked up but said nothing.

"I'm sorry," said Flick.

Charlie didn't respond. Instead, he concentrated on separating his chicken from his potatoes and other vegetables. Soon all the different elements of his dinner were in neat, distinct areas. Even the peas and carrots were piled up in sections so that they didn't touch. Flick watched while he skewered a piece of carrot and examined it as if it were a rare work of art.

"I'm sorry I didn't help you work out Saanvi's trick," she said. "I was just confused because I wanted to find my dad, but I realize now that we really need to win this competition.

I've got so much to tell you about what happened last night. You and I need to start taking it very seriously."

Charlie finally popped the carrot in his mouth. "I've been taking it seriously all along," he mumbled.

"And you were right to. I'm really sorry; I should have listened to you."

"You promised you would think about the trick, you know."

"I shouldn't have broken my promise. That was wrong of me. It won't happen again."

"Good," said Charlie. "Because we've got a lot of work to do if we want to win."

"I'm listening. What do I need to do differently?"

Charlie looked over the top of his glasses at her. "Really?"

"Yes, I'm being serious. Hit me with it."

"OK. You need to be in less of a hurry, not so obsessed with finding your dad. Be more—"

Flick opened her mouth to interrupt.

Charlie held up his hand. "I thought you were listening for once?"

"Sorry." Flick mimed zipping her mouth shut.

"You need to be more in the moment. Enjoy the journey, not just about the destination; live in a way—"

"Are you just listing inspirational memes?"

He ignored this. "You need to be more appreciative. Be kinder to those around you. Be more accepting of their faults. Be forgiving towards your father *and* the Fox. Stop thinking that finding your dad is going to solve all your problems. Don't be so focused on finding him that you forget everyone else. Your friends need you too. Like me..." Charlie tailed off and sat back, folding his arms.

Flick looked at him. "Is that it?"

Charlie nodded.

"OK," said Flick slowly. "I'll try, I promise."

"Good." Charlie pushed his glasses back up his nose.

Flick sat back. "In the meantime, there is something I would like your help with. And I promise while we do this to enjoy the journey and not just worry about the destination."

Charlie smiled. "I might have overdone that bit."

"When I was in Lukas's office yesterday," Flick continued, "I discovered something that looked really interesting. Will you come with me to find out what it is?"

"Will it help us win the competition?"

"I think so."

"Then of course."

At that moment, Harry and Ruby walked over to their table.

"These seats are taken," said Charlie but Harry ignored him and plonked himself down. Ruby hovered behind him and gave Flick a small smile.

"I hope you two realize you don't stand any chance of winning," Harry said.

Flick gave him a withering look and shook her head. "You forget," she said. "We've seen you perform tricks before."

"We're on our way to the castle now to film our finale," said Harry, chewing on a chip. "It's so good it will blow your tiny little minds."

"Just wait for ours," retorted Charlie defiantly.

"I find it hard to believe that anyone as limited as *you*" – Harry gestured at Charlie's plate – "someone who can't even cope with carrots touching his potatoes, and someone" – he nodded at Flick – "who can't even walk, will be able to beat us. You two are pathetic."

He stood up. "Come on, Ruby."

Flick and Charlie watched him walk off across the room, Ruby following in his wake.

"How would you like to watch their trick?" asked Flick.

"We'll never get in," said Charlie. "Channel Seven will have the whole castle cordoned off; we won't be allowed near."

"This thing I want your help in finding – I think it will get us in."

Charlie smiled. "Well, in that case, now I'm even more interested. And speaking of final tricks, I have some last-minute instructions here from the Fox."

Charlie reached into his trouser pocket and pulled out a folded-up piece of paper. He handed it to Flick. "What the Fox wants to do seems pretty extreme to me. I mean, it requires you taking some massive risks. I suppose what I'm trying to say is this: if you want to win, you're going to need to trust the Fox. With your life. With your whole future."

Flick opened the piece of paper and read it. Then she read it again, slowly.

"Wow," she murmured.

"Mind if I join you?" asked a voice.

Flick looked up to find Saanvi, sporting a bright purple T-shirt, standing by their table with a tray. Flick hastily tucked the Fox's notes into the pocket of her shorts.

"Shouldn't you have gone home by now?" Flick asked. "Your team lost."

"We did," Saanvi said, sitting down. "I'm not in the competition any more. But my auntie is part of the camera crew, and they've said I can help out. I'm learning how to do camera work, although most of the time I seem to end up just making people tea."

"Cool," said Charlie, suddenly paying particularly close attention to a potato.

"In fact," continued Saanvi, "here come some of my new crew mates now."

"They can have our seats," offered Flick. "We're just going."

Charlie still hadn't looked up.

"Aren't we, Charlie?" Flick raised her eyebrows at him.

Charlie slowly stood up, still with his eyes glued to his plate. He followed Flick across the dining room, where they returned their trays.

"Have you recovered?" Flick asked with a smirk.

"So, what are we looking for?" asked Charlie, changing

the subject hastily as they walked down the corridor to the foyer.

In answer Flick led him out into the square. It was a cloudy, calm evening. Few tourists were around, and the streets were quiet. The cafe tables outside the hotel were empty, umbrellas and tablecloths gently fluttering in the breeze.

"In De Haas's office was a map," said Flick. "And it showed a connection between that fountain over there and the castle keep."

"What do you mean, a connection?"

"Well, that's what I need your help with."

Flick and Charlie examined the stone fountain from all sides. There was a large circular pool and rising from the middle was a three-tiered water feature. Each progressively smaller layer was suspended from a central pillar, allowing the water to cascade from top to bottom and gently splash into the pool. On one side of the fountain was a covered gazebo with a series of stone arches and benches where you could sit and look out across the water.

"So are we looking for a hidden panel?" Charlie asked. "Or a secret entrance?"

"Possibly. The connection might be some sort of tunnel. With the map were descriptions for a trick where the magician gets from here up to the castle quickly."

"Oooh, sounds interesting."

"If you were going to hide a secret entrance to a tunnel here, where would you put it?" asked Flick.

"I'd put it in the gazebo at the back. No leaking, and you could sneak in and not be seen by people passing."

Flick nodded.

They both walked around the side of the fountain and into the gazebo. Here the front wall consisted of arches, but the back was solid stone, and into this had been carved geometric patterns and hunting scenes. Several gargoyles were also dotted about, and these stared out at the fountain with unblinking eyes and pained expressions.

Charlie examined the rear wall, poking it here and there.

"I think you're right," said Flick. "It makes sense to put it somewhere about here." She pulled on a gargoyle. "We need to find the release mechanism."

Charlie spun around slowly, looking at all the details afresh.

"How about this?" he asked. Behind one of the arch supports was a metal pump, perhaps to draw water out of the pool for drinking. It had a rusty handle, and he pulled it up and then down. There was a clunking noise and a section of the relief swung inwards, making Flick jump. She could see some stone steps disappearing down inside.

Charlie grinned. "We make the best team, don't we?"

"We sure do," agreed Flick. "It would be a crime for us not to keep working together."

"Is that a promise?" Charlie asked.

"It is."

Charlie stepped into the darkness and Flick followed.

29
The Ride

Inside the door was a glowing button. Charlie pressed it and the door shut behind them. At the same time, some strip lights pinged dimly into life on the ceiling above, allowing them to make out the steep set of steps that disappeared down into a long brick tunnel. Charlie took Flick's hand and they slowly edged forward. The bricks that made up the arched tunnel were old and had been stained black or rusty orange here and there by water damage. Thankfully the steps were in good condition.

When they arrived at the bottom, they found themselves on a short concrete platform with a railway running alongside. The area was lit with more of the dull strip lights. There was a set of buffers on the right and the track disappeared into a black tunnel on the left. In front of them was a short pillar with another glowing button on top.

"Shall I?" asked Charlie, his hand hovering over it.

Flick smiled. "Of course."

He pressed the button. At first, nothing happened and then gradually they could hear a faint rumbling coming down the tracks. As the noise got louder, it was joined by the higher notes of squealing wheels, and eventually something resembling a roller coaster glided into the station. It consisted of three little red cars, each big enough for two people to sit side by side on a bench. It pulled to a stop in front of the platform and gently nudged the buffers.

Flick and Charlie got into the front carriage, furthest from the buffers, and pulled a metal safety bar down over them.

Flick grinned. "Shall I?" she asked, holding her hand over another glowing button set into the dashboard.

Charlie laughed. "Of course. How cool is this?"

Flick pressed the button and the little train lurched forward. Quickly building up speed, it flew into the black tunnel. It was impossible to tell how fast they were going because they couldn't see anything, but the wind blew Flick's hair all over her face as their carriage lurched left and right. Eventually a disc of light became visible ahead, and as the train started to slow, they burst out of the tunnel and arrived at another station that looked identical to the one they had left. The train gently nudged up against a similar set of buffers.

Flick and Charlie pushed the safety bar up and climbed out. In place of the steps that had led down to the first platform, here there was a lift. They pressed the single button and the silver doors slid open.

"The lift must cut through the rock the castle sits on," Charlie said as they stepped inside and pressed the button to ascend.

Flick nodded. "Good job there aren't more stairs."

They rose higher and higher.

"When I rule the world," Flick said, "I shall decree that there be more lifts."

Charlie grinned. "I'll be sure to look out for that."

At the top, they stepped out into a small space with bare concrete walls, floor and ceiling. There was another glowing button, which they pressed, and one wall slowly opened.

Flick recognized the hallway of the castle keep immediately. The opening was disguised as a wooden panel just behind one of the suits of armour, and they slipped through into the hallway. They crept forward towards the great hall.

"Well, that was interesting," whispered Charlie.

They peeked cautiously round the door. The great hall was full of people sitting on chairs watching Harry and Ruby on the stage. They looked like they were just about to start their trick.

Charlie smiled. "This should be fun."

30

The Great Hope

Flick and Charlie slipped silently into the back of the great hall. Dominic Drake was standing on the stage wearing a microphone headset, talking to the crowd. On the right were Harry and Ruby, and in the middle of the stage was a wooden bench.

"I need a member of the audience to participate in our trick today," Drake announced, raising one arm and pointing at the spectators. "Ruby, I would like you to close your eyes and in a moment say stop. Whenever you like." He started to swing his arm from right to left.

"Stop!" Ruby shouted after a pause. Drake froze.

"The lady wearing the blue checked shirt," he said. "Yes, you, madam. Stand up, please. Could you come up to the stage?"

The woman nodded and began to weave her way through the audience.

"Now, we've asked Noah from Synergy to join us; he's going to be sitting on this bench."

Drake gestured to a long wooden seat in the centre of the stage as Noah walked on in his shiny metallic blue shell suit to a loud cheer. He sat down in the middle of the bench and gave everyone a wave.

"And now," said Drake, "I'll hand over to Harry."

Harry strode forward confidently. "Right, Noah was our competitor, so you know he won't be doing anything to help us. Will you, Noah?"

"No way!" exclaimed Noah, laughing.

The woman had now made her way up the steps onto the stage and Harry beckoned her over. "I'm going to try and guess your name," said Harry. He squinted. "I think ... your first name is Sara. Am I correct?"

The woman nodded.

"And your surname begins with ... a J. In fact, I think it's Johnson. Is that right? Sara Johnson?"

The woman nodded again and looked impressed.

"Now, I have here a pen and a piece of blank paper which I'm going to give you. Take a look at Noah sitting on that bench. I want you to imagine what he might be looking at. He's there to enjoy the view of a famous landmark somewhere in the world. And I also want you to imagine what day of the week he might be looking at this landmark, and at what time of day. So think of a landmark, day of the week and time of day, and write all that on this piece of paper. Make it as random as you like."

The woman nodded as Ruby handed her the pen. Ruby then held up the paper to the audience, showing both sides as blank, before passing this to the woman as well.

The woman took the paper and began to write. "Finished," she said, after a moment.

"OK, if you would like to read out what you've written, please," said Harry.

"I've written *Eiffel Tower, Wednesday* and *sixteen minutes past eleven*."

"Sixteen minutes past eleven. That's very specific. I like it! A big round of applause for Sara Johnson!"

The crowd cheered and whooped.

"If you can now hold up the paper so the camera can see it," said Harry. "And, Noah, if you could just move a little to your left."

Noah shuffled down the seat to reveal a brass plaque in the middle of the bench. On it was engraved:

This seat is dedicated to Noah,
who likes to sit here and look at the Eiffel Tower
on a Wednesday at sixteen minutes past eleven.

The crowd erupted in even louder cheers.

Flick and Charlie took this opportunity to sneak back

out of the great hall. The hallway was still deserted so they walked the short distance to the suit of armour unnoticed and slipped behind it. There was a glowing button on the wall. Flick pressed it and the wooden panel sprang open, exposing the silver lift doors. They pressed the call button and the doors slid open. They stepped quickly inside.

"That was a pretty awesome trick!" admitted Charlie as the doors shut and the lift descended. "I don't know how they did that. And yet the performance itself was so simple. I'm now worried our trick is too complicated. What if we mess it up? And even if we don't mess it up, it still might not have the same level of impact as theirs because there are so—"

Flick held up her hand. "Don't worry. Our trick will be amazing." She patted his shoulder reassuringly.

Charlie looked doubtful. "Well, at least we're all now pulling in the same direction; you, me and the Fox – we do work really well together."

"Well, you and me at least," said Flick. "I still don't trust the Fox. I agree we need to help him win this competition, and I'm going to give it my best shot. But I still worry about what he's really up to. I do believe he wants to stop Drake and De Haas, and he's right about that, but what's his goal beyond? I still think he's using us."

"You might be right," agreed Charlie. "But we can only base our decisions on what we know for certain. Sometimes you can't worry about what's beyond that."

Flick smiled. "You're getting to be almost wise in your old age."

Charlie laughed. "I'll tell you what I *have* learnt. While you've been busy practising your lock picking and box switching, I've been doing some research up at the castle, and apparently the diamond necklace in the vault is called the Great Hope. That's what the mural in town is all about. The story goes that once upon a time the baker of Linth had a beautiful daughter. Although they were very poor she had many suitors, but then she caught the eye of the old king of Linth. His wife had recently died, and he was seeking a new bride. The king tried to woo the baker's daughter and held lavish parties at the castle to impress her. But she wasn't interested in marrying the king. So he gave her a diamond necklace and she was so struck by its beauty that she agreed to accept his proposal. As soon as they were married, he locked her away in the castle tower and she was only seen whenever they announced the birth of another child."

"Not a very happy ending," said Flick.

They arrived on the platform where the train was still waiting for them, and climbed in.

"No, it's a bit sad, isn't it?" muttered Charlie.

"So the necklace was a trick?"

"I thought you'd enjoy the irony."

"A trick used by the old king to trap the baker's daughter," Flick mused.

"That's how the story goes."

"That plan you gave me earlier from the Fox, that was quite something," she said. "Unless we're also being fooled by the Great Hope."

"Yes," said Charlie slowly.

"Then we'd better talk it through and work out all the details."

"I'm all ears."

Flick hit the button and the train lurched forward into the tunnel.

31
The Moves

The next day was Friday – the day of the trick. Later on, it would be time to get into character, but first the Fox's new instructions for Flick were to practise how her moves combined with those of Gemma and Charlie. It was important for them to know one another's roles inside out as well as their own, so Charlie marked out an exact map on the ballroom floor in tape to show the vault, the corridor and the lift area. This was where the space of the ballroom came into its own, as Flick, Charlie and Gemma practised walking through their various positions and sequences until they had fixed the logic of the trick firmly in their minds. When they had finished, they knew by heart where they each needed to be at all times.

At the end of the morning, Flick practised picking the lock

another twenty times. She could now get the drawer open in less than a minute every time. It felt great to be part of a team, perfecting their intricate moves, honing the choreography, building towards the rush of a performance. This was why she loved magic. Flick was buzzing and even Gemma looked like she was nearly enjoying herself.

For part of the trick Flick and Charlie would need to wear disguises, and after lunch it was time to try them out. Gemma took Flick and Charlie up to her room, and Kevin the cameraman stood guard outside the door to ensure they weren't disturbed. Flick sat down in front of a large mirror and Gemma went to work. She started off adding layers of putty to Flick's nose, building it up more and more until it looked suitably aquiline. Then she added a blonde wig over the top of Flick's brown hair. The wig was made of real hair and looked very realistic. The final flourish was to give Flick blue contact lenses.

By the time Gemma had finished, Flick was pretty sure that her own mother wouldn't have recognized her. She stared at herself in the mirror, fascinated, while Gemma began work on Charlie. When he was finally ready, Flick couldn't stop laughing. Charlie looked like an old man. He even started to act the part, shuffling about with a stoop. It was an incredible transformation until he got the giggles, and then he returned to being quite obviously Charlie.

One look at Gemma's face soon stopped the laughter, and

she began the laborious process of removing the putty and make-up. The Fox had insisted they practise everything, even their disguises, and this dry run had been a grand success. It took a good half-hour before Charlie and Flick were back to normal, and while Gemma was working away, the pair of them discussed Team Drake's trick.

"Well," said Charlie. "Once the trick started, nothing could have happened to that bench or Noah would have noticed, and nothing gets past him. So it makes no sense."

Flick thought hard while Gemma removed her wig. "Even if they worked out what the woman was writing, there was no way they could have got it on that plaque. It was genuinely engraved."

"Hmm. Ouch!" cried Charlie as Gemma tugged his wig off.

"If you sit still, it will be easier," complained Gemma.

"The only way it could have been done," continued Fick, "is if the audience member was a plant."

Charlie nodded. "Exactly. And we know that's against the rules."

"I said keep still!" Gemma demanded crossly.

When the disguises were finally off, Flick and Charlie returned to the ballroom. This time they introduced a further element: two production cases, which were large black metal boxes on wheels for transporting TV equipment. The two cases they would use in the trick each contained a camera, a tripod, a laptop and some cables. Both boxes appeared identical, with hinged lids that opened on top. But one of them had been modified by the Fox and had a small hidden compartment in the side. This could be accessed, when the lid was open, by pressing a very small button on the bottom of the case. The button looked and felt like a rivet, and would only reveal the sliding panel when pressed in exactly the right way.

Because line of sight was critical for this part of the trick, the three of them practised their positions again and again. Kevin joined them, playing the part of a bank guard. He stood and watched each performance carefully to see if he could spot anything suspicious. Every movement they made had to flow and look perfectly natural.

Gemma positioned box one on a prearranged spot. Flick opened the lid of box two and ducked down behind it as if using the laptop. She plugged a cable into the camera which then needed to be connected to the laptop in the box. As she did this, she started to whistle: a signal to Gemma. On the signal, Gemma dropped the camera onto the laptop in box one, causing a distraction. Flick then quickly knelt down beside box two, pressed the hidden button and slid open the panel to expose the compartment. Charlie talked to Kevin about what had happened to try to keep his attention away from Flick.

Then came the moment when Flick got her minute to pick the lock. The lines of sight and timing were crucial so they practised it again and again until they could do it in their sleep.

By mid-afternoon Flick had well and truly had enough. She knew the plan, she knew the moves, but did she want to go through with it? It would all require complete trust in the Fox, and she didn't know if she had that. There would come a point where she would have to commit, a moment where there would be no going back. That time was fast approaching.

32
The Fight Back

Later that afternoon they would need to go to the bank to set up the trick, but until then, Flick and Charlie finally had time to get some rest.

As they made their way upstairs Flick said, "In a few hours, we'll be filming the trick and then this competition will all be over. We need to make sure we get this right."

"I know," said Charlie.

"When things kick off ... you're going to need to talk to Saanvi."

"Me?" Charlie looked panicked.

"Yes, you."

"But I can't talk to girls."

"You talk to me."

"But you're…"

"Not a girl?"

"Different," he said slowly.

"How?"

"I can't talk to Saanvi. My brain turns to mush."

"Seriously!" Flick exclaimed. "We don't have time for this. I have to go and do my thing, so you need to go and do yours. It's vital for the trick."

Charlie looked genuinely terrified. "But how do I talk to her?"

"Just be you. Just chill."

"I don't think I can."

Flick sighed. "The big secret, Charlie, is that none of us know how to talk to people. We're all in the same boat just having a go. She's no different from anyone else."

Charlie thought about this for a while. "I guess it would help if I viewed it that way," he admitted. Then he lowered his glasses and looked at Flick over the top of them. "You're getting to be almost wise in your old age."

Flick smiled. "I just think that you need to live in the moment more. Be less worried about the destination. Enjoy the journey of talking to Saanvi."

Charlie laughed and slid his glasses back up his nose. "I'll have a go," he said as they parted company on the landing.

Flick closed the door of her room and climbed onto the bed. She propped the pillow up and lay back against it, closing her eyes. It felt good to take the weight off her limb, but she couldn't relax. Her mind was spinning with all that they had to do.

Eventually she gave up trying to rest and decided to get some fresh air. She made her way back downstairs, across the car park and wandered into the Team Fox base, not really sure where else to go. She turned on the lights, sat herself down in one of the armchairs in front of the fake fire and went over the plan again and again in her mind.

Was she really going to do this? What choice did she have?

Hello, Flick.

The voice sounded even deeper than before. Trying not to flinch, she kept her eyes firmly shut and focused on looking completely relaxed.

You're going to be thrown out of the competition.

Flick didn't respond.

You saw Drake bribe the council members; they'll do what he asks. You don't stand a chance.

She twisted her head around slowly, trying to pinpoint where the voice was coming from. Was it the Team Fox logo?

You remember I told you about the painting?

She squinted, trying to focus. Not the logo. Somewhere nearer.

Did the Fox talk to you about it?

Flick waited.

I thought not.

She stood up and stepped slowly towards the table.

He hasn't been honest with you about why he wants it.

Could the voice be coming from the chandelier? She pulled one of the chairs out from under the table and climbed up onto it, examining the light fitting.

He knows where your dad is, and he's not going to tell you. He's also going to stand by and let you get arrested for the theft of the painting. Once he knows what's on the back of it. That's the information he's after. You want to see your dad again? Well, once you're in prison you'll never see any of your family again.

Flick started to unscrew the fitting.

"I'll tell you what I do know," she said slowly. "I know you are Lukas De Haas." The fitting came away and she opened it up. "I know you have CCTV all over this town and because this is your hotel, you have cameras and speakers installed wherever you like."

The fitting had a brass bottom which she examined. There was a very small speaker nestled inside it with some wires and a little black box.

"I know that you want the real Bell System," she continued, speaking into the box. "And you'll destroy anything and anyone in your way. Including me, if you get the chance. I also know that you're a coward, which is why you hide behind this stupid voice. And I know that I don't trust a single word you say."

She pulled the wires one by one out of the box and the speaker until she held a collection of disconnected bits in her hand. She stepped down off the chair and dropped them on the floor.

Then she proceeded to stamp on them with her good foot, again and again and again until they were crushed.

33
The Set-Up

At four o'clock, as prearranged, Gemma banged on Flick's door, and Flick woke up with a start. She must have finally dozed off. She tried to shake herself awake as Gemma bustled in with her make-up bags. It was time to get ready.

"Sit," Gemma ordered.

Flick sat and Gemma went to work. She built the contours of her nose up and artfully arranged the blonde wig. Finally Flick inserted the blue contact lenses before pulling on a baseball cap to shield her face. The black overalls hid her prosthetic nicely and the cap and disguise did the same for her face.

"Let's go," was all Gemma said as they left the room and marched down to the foyer where "old" Charlie was waiting for them, practising his stoop. Flick got the giggles again.

He said, "I've always wanted to know what I've got to look forward to. Although I'm not sure I—"

"In the van," barked Gemma.

A Channel Seven van was parked outside the front entrance, and Flick and Charlie got in the back while Gemma drove them up the hill to the bank. When they pulled up outside it was a little after five thirty and the bank had just shut. They parked outside the main entrance and were met at the door by two security guards, who checked their photo ID cards to confirm they were members of the TV crew. Flick and Charlie produced fake ones with aliases and photos of their new faces. The guards then looked inside the van to make sure there was nothing suspicious in the back. Little did they know, thought Flick. When they were satisfied everything seemed OK, the guards gave them the all-clear to unload.

Gemma and Flick set up a ramp on the back of the van and wheeled the two production cases out, Flick remembering to keep her baseball cap pulled down low over her eyes. Then Charlie moved the ramp and they wheeled the cases into the bank's foyer. The two guards followed them closely, watching every move they made.

Anyone would think they were expecting a robbery.

The guards opened the doors to the right of the cashier stations so the trio could make their way into the back area. Before they were allowed to enter, however, they had to submit to a thorough search. The guards started with the equipment, making them unpack everything. Both production cases contained a camera and a tripod. One set was to be left in the vault; the other was a spare. The cameras were wrapped in black polystyrene protective foam, and the guards removed this and felt all around the inside of the cases.

Both cases also contained a laptop and a selection of cables, and they asked Gemma to turn the laptops on to prove they were real. They examined them from all sides and then looked at the outside and underneath of the boxes before finally turning their attention to Flick, Charlie and Gemma themselves. They were patted down very thoroughly and even asked to remove their shoes. Flick was very careful to hide her prosthetic foot by removing her shoes with her back to the guards and then keeping her plastic foot behind her real one at all times. She had socks on so it would pass a cursory glance, but the guards never actually looked down. They were so busy examining all the shoes for secret compartments it didn't seem to occur to them to check their feet as well.

When the guards were finally satisfied, the lift doors were opened from the control room and Charlie and Gemma wheeled the cases inside. They all descended to the basement and stepped out into the service corridor.

At this point, the guards insisted they split up – only one person was allowed in the vault at a time. Gemma and Charlie stayed with the case containing the spare camera and tripod at the lift end of the service corridor, and Flick carried on to the vault. She wheeled her case along behind the two guards, towards the door, where they both typed in their eight-digit codes and the door slowly swung open.

As it opened, the lights pinged on inside revealing the vault.

Flick was in. Now she could really get started.

34
The Point of No Return

Flick pushed the case carefully into the vault and took in her surroundings. The black box containing the diamonds was sitting on the glass table, and deposit boxes lined the walls. She silently counted the boxes from the left twice to double-check she had the right one, and then she casually pushed the case across the floor until it was positioned in the correct spot – on the right-hand side of the vault, sideways on to the door and right in front of the correct safety deposit box. While she was doing this, one guard walked back down the service corridor to keep an eye on Gemma and Charlie; the other one remained by the vault door and watched Flick.

Flick lifted the hinged lid of the production case, creating an effective screen, but she didn't move into the space behind the case yet, so as not to draw attention to it. Misdirection would be very important in the next few minutes.

Next Flick reached into the case and lifted out the tripod, which she carried to the front right corner of the vault and set up ready for the camera. She then returned to the case and carefully lifted out the camera, bringing it over to the tripod. With the camera successfully on the tripod, she looked through the viewfinder. It had a perfect view of the black box containing the diamonds on the table. She double-checked that it would also film the deposit box door and be able to see deep inside, once it was open.

Then she pressed record. Everything from this moment on would be captured for the show.

Everything.

Flick walked back to the open production case and took out a cable. She plugged one end of the cable into the laptop and then walked over to the camera and connected the other end to it. The laptop inside the production case and camera were now linked. This did nothing – it was completely for show, all part of the routine they'd designed to make the guard see a drawn-out series of actions to set up the camera. If the sequence was long enough, then no single moment would stand out.

Or so they hoped.

Flick now moved into the shielded space behind the production case and bent over as if to use the laptop. As she leant forward behind the upright lid, she disappeared from the guard's view. At this point, she started to whistle while she tapped away on the laptop.

This was the prearranged signal to Gemma. She hoped that Gemma and Charlie had been busy getting their laptop and camera out of their case, pretending to check their spare equipment.

A few seconds after Flick started to whistle, she heard a huge crash. Gemma had dropped her camera on the laptop and both items had fallen onto the floor.

Flick started to count the seconds in her head.

The guard by the vault door turned to see the cause of all the commotion.

Flick immediately pressed the button underneath the production case and the hidden side panel opened. She got out her lock picking tools from the compartment and then spun round to face the deposit box door. She worked away, all too aware of time slipping by. Thankfully she had it open in just over thirty seconds. All that practice had paid off.

She peered inside. Sure enough, the box was empty. She checked that the camera could see into the vacant space, counted a couple of seconds in her head so that there was a good amount of footage, and then clicked the door shut again.

She stood up and strolled over to the camera, as casually as she could. She had timed it just right; the guard was now watching her again. Flick stood with her back to the guard to block his line of sight and put both hands on the camera as if checking it was secure. In reality she was sliding a small black box, identical to the one the diamonds were in, out of the back of the camera. She then turned to face the guard and slipped the dummy box into the secret pouch in her overalls. She walked around the vault as if checking the angles for the camera, pausing in front of the box on the glass table.

Right on cue, Charlie shuffled up the service corridor to apologize for the noise and to explain what had happened. Flick's guard turned towards him and held up a hand to stop him, explaining that he had to remain at the far end of the corridor. Only one person was allowed in the vault at a time, he reminded him. Charlie apologized profusely again and shuffled noisily back down the corridor.

While this was going on, Flick pushed the dummy box out of the pouch on her back and placed it on the table behind her. She then quickly slid it into the centre of the table while pulling the real box towards her, and then in one smooth action picked this up and slipped it into the pouch. The whole sequence took about two seconds and looked like her shoulder was sore, and to help this she was just stretching her arm behind her.

Flick then walked away from the table and over to the production case to turn off the laptop and disconnect the cable. Facing the guard, she nudged the box with the diamonds out of the pouch in her overalls and then hid it behind the cable as she rolled it up. She disconnected the other end of the cable from the camera. As she did this, she put herself between the camera and the guard with her back to him. Using her body to hide her actions, she pushed the black box into the empty slot on the camera.

The two boxes had now been switched; the diamonds were in the camera.

Flick then returned to the production case and stowed the cables inside and closed the lid. She allowed herself a small sigh of relief before she wheeled the case out of the vault. The guard swung the door shut behind her and it was locked.

Out in the corridor Flick was reunited with Charlie and Gemma and the second guard and they all travelled back up in the lift to the ground floor. There they had to endure another thorough search. Both production cases had to be emptied again. Flick's case now held only cables and a laptop; the other one contained a broken laptop and camera, a tripod and some cables. All the packing foam was again removed and carefully checked.

Charlie, Gemma and Flick were all patted down and searched. Their shoes were examined last, and once again Flick kept her prosthetic foot tucked behind the other one, but just like the first time the guards didn't look down. Finally, they were allowed to wheel the two cases back down the corridor, through the security doors, across the main foyer and out to the van. Trying not to grin, they quickly loaded the cases, climbed in and drove sedately away.

Job done.

35
The Persuasion

Across town, Victor Odermatt had been at his desk for hours already. He had a new suspicious death to investigate, and the drug trafficking case was going badly. He needed more people. He needed more coffee.

His phone buzzed and he pressed the intercom button.

"Yes," he muttered.

"Someone calling himself the Great Fox is here to see you, sir."

Oh, joy.

Victor sighed. "Send him through."

What made someone call himself the Great Fox? The ego! Maybe he should order everyone to call him the Great Detective.

The door swung open and in walked a man wearing a large fox mask.

Victor looked him up and down. "And you must be…" He feigned glancing down at his notes. "The Great Badger?"

"My name is the Fox."

"Really? That's a surprise. And how can I help you, Mr Fox?"

"I don't know if you're aware, but two apprentices under my instruction are due to perform a magic trick at the De Haas Bank tonight at half past nine."

"I believe I have heard something about it."

"But I think there may be a problem. I think one of them might be planning to use it as a cover for a real theft."

Victor nodded. "Right. I see. Yet you say you are the one responsible for planning this trick?"

"Yes."

"So you're telling me that one of the apprentices you've chosen to steal some diamonds is a thief?"

"Might be planning something. Might be a thief."

"Is this person not supposed to be following your instructions?"

"Yes."

"So you have no control over them?"

"She's just a kid who's upset about her dad. It's a long story but she's pretty mixed up and sometimes kids do crazy things."

Victor nodded again. "And do you have any actual evidence for this planned theft?"

"I can do better than that. I can supply you with a photo of her. I have already told you when the theft will take place. And I can tell you that the whole thing will be recorded by a camera inside the vault, so all the evidence you need will be captured on film."

"And I can see this film?"

"Of course."

"Very well. Leave it with me. Now if you will excuse me, I have other matters to attend to."

The Fox nodded and walked out, closing the door behind him.

Victor sighed and stared up at the ceiling. Weighing up the details, he grabbed the phone. "Get me Detective Koehl on the line."

There was a pause while he was connected. Then he said, "Leo, what are you doing tonight?"

There was a pause while Leo answered.

Then Victor said, "Good. Because we have a magic trick to watch."

36
The Start

Victor and Leo arrived at the bank and walked into the foyer. A woman with pink hair, a nose ring and a grumpy face approached them. Her badge said *Gemma is happy to help*. Someone had drawn a line through the word *happy* with a black marker pen.

"Are you guys here for—" she began.

"My name is Victor Odermatt. I'm Linth's chief of police and this is Detective Leo Koehl. We are here to observe the filming of tonight's trick."

"Oh." Gemma looked surprised. "Well, follow me then," she said and led them across the foyer. A security guard opened the door to the right of the cashier stations. There they walked down a corridor, through another door and up some stairs.

"The police are here," Gemma announced as they stepped out through a fire exit onto a flat roof.

The Fox and Lukas De Haas were standing next to each other, ready to start filming. The Fox was wearing a black suit and a white shirt; De Haas was dressed in a black shirt, dark red silk waistcoat and matching trousers which billowed like sails in the breeze.

All around them the TV crew were busy getting everything into position. They all paused and turned to look at Victor and Leo as they stepped onto the roof.

"I can assure you that we are here simply to observe," Victor said loudly. "Please continue."

The Fox nodded, and he and De Haas went back to facing each other.

"OK. All set?" asked one of the crew.

Everyone was ready.

"Action."

The Fox spoke first. "Good evening. I'm the Great Fox, and tonight we're going to attempt the heist of the century – to make twenty-five million euros' worth of diamonds disappear from one of the most secure vaults in the world."

The camera panned round to show the Linth night sky-line, all lit up, before returning to the Fox.

"I'm standing on the roof of one of the oldest and most secure banks in the world, but tonight all that is going to change."

The Fox turned his back on De Haas and strolled across the roof towards the steps. One of the camera crew walked backwards ahead of him, and Victor and Koehl moved hastily out of his way. As he started down the steps, the Fox delivered his lines straight down.

"For the past three hundred years the De Haas Bank has kept its clients' valuables safe. It has never had a break-in. Until tonight."

37
The End

Much later, when they'd finished filming, the Fox popped some champagne. Everyone was on a high. It's always hard to be certain when you are involved in performing a trick how it will look to an audience, but the crew seemed pretty sure they'd made some sensational TV, ready to be shown in the great hall at the grand finale the following evening. The Fox went around shaking everyone's hand and slapping people on the back, convinced he'd done enough to be the next chancellor.

Flick mingled with the crew for a bit, but she wasn't really in the mood for partying. She kept thinking about what was about to happen, hoping she had prepared well enough, knowing it wouldn't be pleasant. The Fox always said that ninety per cent of a good trick was in the preparation. Had she done enough? Their final trick was indeed impressive and was likely to win him the chancellorship, but could he be trusted with it? Only time would tell.

She caught Charlie's eye, and they headed outside to the TV vans that were parked in the castle courtyard.

"Now, remember," said Flick. "You're going to have to do this bit on your own. Are you ready?"

Charlie nodded. "Yes, I think so."

Flick hung back and watched Charlie walk towards a row of Channel Seven vans. Several of the crew were loading equipment into the back of the first one.

"Is Saanvi about?" Charlie asked.

"Next van," grunted one, so Charlie kept walking along the line.

Saanvi, currently in a yellow T-shirt, was sitting in an editing suite at the back of the van listening to a sound engineer.

Charlie saw Saanvi and froze. Flick watched him open his mouth but could hear that nothing was coming out of it. She willed him forward. *Come on, Charlie!*

The engineer spotted Charlie and tapped Saanvi on the shoulder.

"I think someone is here to see you," he said, smirking.

Saanvi looked up and smiled.

"Hi, Charlie," she said, stepping out of the van.

"Hi, Saanvi," said Charlie.

Flick saw Charlie take a deep breath. "I wonder if you could help us out with something. We need to borrow a camera."

"Borrow one?"

"Yes, for one final trick."

Saanvi frowned. "They are very expensive. If anything happened to one of them, I would be in a *lot* of trouble with Channel Seven."

"But what if we borrowed one with an operator who would look after it and use it properly? An operator like Kevin, perhaps. It won't take long."

"How long?"

"Just a couple of hours. We really need Kevin's help – just for a little bit. And I thought, since you're in with the camera crew, you could ask for us."

Saanvi smiled. "Seeing as it's you asking... I'll see what I can do."

Flick watched and smiled to herself. Charlie would be just fine.

And then she saw the blue lights reflected in the side of the van.

She turned to see two police officers get out of their car and walk towards her.

"Are you Felicity Lions?" one of the police officers asked.

Flick nodded nervously.

"We'd like you to accompany us to the police station."

PART FOUR

Consequences

In which the magician builds
towards the finale. Can the impossible
be made possible? Either way,
there's no going back now.

38
The Arrest

The two officers marched Flick through the narrow entrance into the cramped foyer of Linth police station. There was another police officer behind the glass of the reception desk, and as Flick was propelled towards her, she said something in German.

Flick looked at her blankly.

"*Englisch*," replied one of the officers accompanying Flick.

"You speak English?" the officer behind the glass asked her.

Flick nodded.

The officer disappeared through a door and returned a few minutes later with a male colleague. He had quite a bit of gold braid on his uniform and was holding a printout of a photo of Flick. He looked at the photo, then up at Flick, then back down at the photo again, and up at Flick for a second time. Finally, he held the printout up against the glass, so it was next to Flick's face. Flick could see the photo had been taken when they had been filming on the roof of the bakery. How tired and bedraggled must she be looking to make identification this difficult?

There was quite a bit of muttering in German at this point and a number of phone calls were made while Mr Gold Braid stood and pointed at Flick. Perhaps he would be rewarded with more gold braid because of this sterling work in identifying her. He did point particularly well. She wondered if his arm would eventually be covered in so much gold braid it would become too heavy to use. Maybe that's what happened to old police officers in Switzerland, she mused – they didn't retire; they just became weighed down with success to the point where they could no longer usefully serve the community.

After the muttering, and the phoning, Mr Gold Braid formally arrested Flick. He took her purse, watch and belt, and placed them in a box. An inventory of all the items were made which Flick had to sign and date. She was then taken to a side room where she was photographed, and her fingerprints taken. It was then explained to her that she had to sign another piece of paper saying they were her fingerprints.

Once all the relevant paperwork was completed, two more officers appeared to take Flick to a small holding cell.

These two were an interesting double act: one must have been under five foot and the other was well over six feet tall. Flick decided to nickname them Tiny and Tall. Neither of them, Flick noticed, had any gold braid.

Tiny and Tall led Flick down a corridor, Tiny on one side of her and Tall on the other. The floor was scuffed and worn, and there were what looked like scratch marks all along the walls. Eventually they arrived at the cell and the door was politely held open by Tall. The space beyond was about three metres square and contained a built-in bench. Flick stepped inside and sat down on the bench while Tiny and Tall stayed in the corridor.

The room smelt of disinfectant and the yellow walls here were even more worn and damaged. There was a single dull light bulb hanging from the centre of the ceiling in a metal cage. It was the most depressing room Flick had ever seen.

Tall beamed at Flick. "As you are magician, we watch very closely." Tiny guffawed.

Tall was just shutting the door when Tiny stopped him.

"Wait," Tiny said. He stepped into the cell and beckoned Flick over. "Come see. Come see."

Flick got up from the bench. Tiny held out his phone and played a video.

Flick could see Christina standing outside the De Haas Bank. She pursed her lips and put on her most serious face before announcing, "In a shocking twist this evening, the council of the Global Order of Magic have temporarily suspended Team Fox from the competition. Flick and Charlie had chosen the vault at the De Haas Bank for the location of their final trick, which took place earlier this evening. But there is evidence to suggest that this trick might have been a cover for a daring theft. Felicity Lions is currently helping the police with their inquiries. This means that, as things stand, there is only one team left in the competition, and that is Team Drake.

"We are waiting for final confirmation, but if Team Fox are expelled from this competition, then Dominic Drake and his two apprentices, brother and sister act Harry and Ruby Townsend, will automatically be declared the winners. There's never a dull moment here in Linth. I'll get back to you as soon as I know anything further."

Tiny giggled. "It's the end for you," he said, putting his phone away and stepping out of the cell.

"Game over," sneered Tall as he slammed the door shut.

And with that, Flick was all alone. That was it – she had given her all. She'd bet everything she had on the Fox's plan.

She lay back on the rock-hard bench and was frustrated to feel tears sliding down her cheeks. She had spent so much of herself chasing her dad, tried so hard to find him, abandoned her mum so that she was no better than he was, followed him halfway around the world, risked everything. And for what?

Waves of panic washed over her. What if she had got this all wrong?

39
The Interview

Flick was woken by shouting and screaming. She sat up, terrified, as she frantically tried to remember where she was. Slowly her mind started to make sense of the commotion – a man had been placed in the cell next door, and he was either drunk or angry. Possibly both. Flick lay back listening to him shouting and kicking at the walls. After about an hour or two, he quietened down and she tried to get back to sleep, but it was no use.

At long last she was brought some breakfast. A tray was pushed through a hatch in the door, where it sat on a little shelf. The bread was like cardboard, and the margarine they'd spread on it tasted like plastic, but Flick didn't care. She was starving.

Some time later, Tiny and Tall returned and led her out of the cell and down another grimy corridor to an interview room. The room had grey walls, a grey ceiling and a grey floor, and Flick sat down on a grey chair at a grey table. At one end of the table was a grey tape machine. The only thing that wasn't grey was the large mirror on one wall, which Flick guessed was mirrored glass. She wondered how many people had queued up on the other side to watch her interview.

Two men entered the room. The first had grey hair and a grey goatee beard. He'd clearly decorated the room. He sat down opposite Flick and pressed record on the tape machine.

He said, "My name is Victor Odermatt. I'm Linth's chief of police and this is Detective Leo Koehl."

The other man remained standing behind him. He had blond hair, glasses and the stooped posture and squint of an academic. He was younger and less physically imposing than Odermatt, and it was obvious he was more junior.

Odermatt continued. "You are being interviewed over the theft of a painting from a safety deposit box in the De Haas Bank. I'm conducting this interview in English so you can understand. Is this OK?"

Flick nodded.

"Could you speak for the benefit of the tape?"

"Yes."

"Do you understand the accusation of theft from the De Haas Bank?"

"Yes, I understand."

"Were you involved in the magic trick that took place at the bank last night?"

"Yes, I was."

"We are obliged under Swiss law to inform you that you are currently the prime suspect in our investigations of the theft of the painting. Do you understand?"

"Yes. I understand."

"We are conducting a detailed fingerprint analysis of the vault and collecting evidence. I have to say, at this early stage, it's not looking good for you. Do you understand that if you are prosecuted here, you will be detained in this country and unable to go home?"

"Yes, I do."

"And if you are found guilty, there is a very high penalty for this crime? We take the security of our banks very seriously indeed."

A uniformed officer poked his head round the door and murmured something in German. Victor nodded and replied briefly.

"Excuse me," he said to Flick. "We will continue this interview shortly."

With that, Victor pressed stop on the tape machine and walked out, followed by Leo.

They were gone for a long time. Flick was left alone to stare at the grey walls and doubt. All magicians were liars and they made you doubt. It was how they earnt a living. While they were busy explaining how solid the box was, how straightforward and honest and trustworthy it was, one of their hands was round the back opening a hidden compartment. Deceit was in their nature.

And yet.

Here she was. Trusting in the Fox's plan. Betting her freedom, her future, everything she had, on what he had promised. She hoped that this box was solid.

When Victor at last returned, he sat back down opposite Flick and sighed.

"Listen, we will soon have footage that shows you were the only one who entered that vault. A Channel Seven employee called Gemma has been questioned and identified you, despite your clever disguise. We've examined all the safety deposit boxes, and we can see the lock of one of them has been tampered with. We've checked the outside of that box and found your fingerprints all over it, particularly around the lock. We've also checked the inside of the deposit box door and found your fingerprints there too. So, we know you broke into it. That is a crime in itself, and you will be charged. And in this deposit box there was a painting that is now missing. Bearing this in mind, I'm going to ask you an important question. How you answer could make a big difference to your future. Is there anything you'd like to tell us, Miss Lions?"

"I didn't steal anything," said Flick, trying to stop her voice from shaking.

"Miss Lions. Is that the best you can do? You should know that the only thing I hate more than magic is having my time wasted. Although here they are the same thing. If you cooperate with us, this process will be easier. I'm going to ask you again. Is there anything you'd like to tell us?"

"I haven't stolen anything."

"You are an intelligent young lady. You don't want to throw away years of your life, do you? Time spent in prison is time you can never get back."

Flick was silent. There was simply nothing more she could say.

After a while, Flick was taken back to her cell by Tiny and Tall. The door slammed shut, and she was left alone again. Back to waiting in a cell. No windows. No clock. Under such circumstances, time started to behave very strangely to the point where it couldn't be trusted. It played tricks.

Near where she lived back home, there were some allotments. For a while, two brothers had lived next door and she used to play with them there. It became their space and they got to know some of the gardeners, most of whom tolerated them reluctantly, but a few warmed to them and left them treats of home-made jams and chutneys in their sheds and greenhouses.

There was one particularly large shed down the end of the allotments, made of rusty corrugated iron. Long abandoned, it had fallen into disrepair, leaving it covered in brambles, and inside, it was full of bugs, spiders and the occasional rat. It became a dare to see who could stay inside the longest. The younger brother managed a few hours in daylight; the older brother managed over four hours after dark. One night, Flick shut herself in with no intention of coming out till the next morning. She wanted to win the dare, of course, but mainly she wanted to prove to herself that she wasn't afraid.

She spent all night in that shed. Spiders and rats came and went but she wasn't going to give up.

During that time she learnt not to be afraid of the dark, but more importantly, she learnt not to be afraid of time. Time will pass; it always does. There is power in patience.

Time did indeed pass, and then Flick found herself back in the interview room. After a few minutes, Victor entered on his own and sat down across the table from her.

"So I'd like to offer you a deal," he said. "Are you open to a deal?"

Flick found herself nodding.

"I know that whatever crimes you have committed, ultimately you aren't the one responsible. You've been tricked and used by the Great Fox. He's the one behind all of this. It's not as if you would have come to Switzerland and robbed a bank on your own initiative. So I'm prepared to cut you a deal. If you can help me collect evidence against the Fox, I will release you. You'll be free to go. In fact, I'll do better than that. If you get me enough evidence to convict the Fox, I'll personally try and find your father. What do you say?"

Flick sat there for a beat. She opened her mouth, but nothing came out. Victor seemed like an honest man, not out to trick her or use her. In contrast to everyone else she had met in Linth, he seemed genuine in his desire to help, and this was such a refreshing thing it touched her heart.

Victor looked at his watch. "I'm afraid I need an answer now."

He was a trustworthy man who actually had the powers and skill to find her dad. All she had to do was betray the Fox – a man who might already have betrayed her. Flick didn't know what to say. There was so much crashing around inside her head it couldn't be put into words.

40
The Deal

Flick sat in her cell and felt the anger rise inside her. Someone else was claiming to be able to help her find her father. Victor was offering to help reunite them, but what was her dad doing? Where was he in all this? What effort was he putting into checking she was all right? It wasn't as if he was offering to ride in and save the day. She wanted to cry but felt too angry to let the tears fall. She had to decide whether or not to trust the Fox. What happened now would be down to her and her alone.

No, she thought, that wasn't quite right. There *was* someone she could always rely on. Charlie. She wasn't alone. The two of them would have to see this through.

Her cell door opened, interrupting her thoughts, and she was surprised to see that Victor himself had come to fetch her this time. He reminded her of their deal. She needed to collect evidence on the Fox, enough to convict him of the theft. If she did that, Victor would let her go. If she didn't, he would carry on collecting evidence against her.

Flick listened to everything that Victor said but she already knew what she had to do. It was down to her and Charlie to make this happen, and there was only one way forward.

Before she could be released, Flick had to sign some paperwork to say she understood this deal and what the implications were for not doing as she was told. She was then given back her purse, belt and watch, and she signed another bit of paper to say that all her belongings had been returned. And then she signed *another* bit of paper to say that she was aware she was being released. Finally, she left the police station and stepped onto the pavement, taking a deep breath.

Freedom.

She checked her watch. It was two in the afternoon. Time and Flick were now on speaking terms. She had survived a night in the rusty shed.

A police car pulled up: Flick's ride home. She got in the back seat next to Victor and they pulled away from the kerb and headed down the hill. No one spoke until they pulled up in the square outside the hotel.

Victor said, "I've arranged for those Channel Seven crew members that you requested to meet us here, and I contacted

Charlie Riley as well. I've filled them in on what you need to do. Don't forget, if you want to remain free and see your dad, get me evidence on the Fox."

Flick nodded. "I understand." She got out and the police car drove away. She watched it disappear and then she turned and walked into the hotel reception.

She had no intention of collecting evidence on the Fox. It was time for her to stand up for herself and put her own plan into action.

Inside, she was met by Charlie and Gemma, along with Saanvi and Kevin, who were both holding cameras.

Charlie hugged her. "It's so good to see you. How was your night as a criminal? Are you OK?"

Flick thought of the sound the cell door had made as it slammed shut and the feeling of being trapped in there all alone.

She shrugged nonchalantly. "I've never filled out so much paperwork."

"Kevin knows what we need to do," Charlie confirmed. "The police phoned him and explained everything. We're ready for this." As he finished, he looked towards the door in shock. "What is *he* doing here?"

Flick turned to see the magician from Synergy ducking into the reception. He was still wearing his metallic blue shell suit.

"The plan has changed," said Flick. "We're not collecting evidence to help the police arrest the Fox. We're sticking to our plan, but Winston's going to help us."

"He is?" said Gemma, regarding him doubtfully.

Winston gave a cheery wave.

"Can he be trusted?" whispered Charlie.

"According to the Fox," said Flick. She was pretty sure Winston had lied about knowing where her father was. He was a snake like the rest of them, but she was gambling that at this moment it suited him to be on her side.

Charlie regarded Winston with scepticism. "But how exactly is he going to help?"

"We need a way to show our film. That's where he comes in."

Winston beamed at them. "I promise to be well behaved."

Flick explained everything. It was her plan and, leaving aside the issue of whether the Fox could be trusted, it was a good one. Well, *good* might not be the best word to use. It was a very high-risk gamble with a small chance of success. Likely to end in disaster. However, and this was the crucial point everyone agreed with, it was the only plan they had.

"So," said Kevin, "we have to roll the die and hope it comes up smelling of roses."

"I don't think," said Gemma sternly, "that you have that expression quite right."

"Actually, it's perfect," said Charlie, "because that's even less likely to happen than throwing a six."

And so they got on with it. Flick and Charlie stood in the foyer and took it in turns to talk to the camera while

Kevin filmed them, reeling off the lines Flick had prepared. They filmed several takes until it was perfect and then Charlie led them outside to the fountain. They made their way around the back and into the gazebo.

"Watch and learn," he said as he lifted the rusty pump handle up and down.

Part of the wall swung inwards to reveal the hidden door.

"Wasn't expecting that," said Kevin.

They descended the steps behind Flick so she could dictate the pace.

"How did you find this?" asked Gemma, something forming on her face that looked almost like a smile.

"Flick found a map in De Haas's office," said Charlie. "It showed a dotted line running across town so we knew something started from this fountain, but we didn't know what it was or how to get into it. So we checked the fountain all over and pulled on the gargoyles and pushed the panels but none of them budged, so then we tried—"

"Edited highlights, Charlie," interrupted Flick. "We worked it out."

They arrived at the underground platform, where the three red carriages were waiting for them. They all climbed in, Flick pressed the button and the train leapt forward into the tunnel.

41
The Distraction

The six of them slipped out from behind the suit of armour. Winston tiptoed down the hallway into the great hall to check the TV screen while the rest of them headed out into the castle courtyard and made for the collection of Channel Seven vans parked in front of the tower.

In the back of the first van, just as they had planned, were several large equipment cases. Wheeling these down a ramp out of the van, they retraced their steps across the courtyard and back into the castle. The hallway was narrow, and the equipment cases took up a lot of room. Leaving them stacked in the hallway, the five returned to the van, collected another set of cases and wheeled these into the hallway too. There was now only a very thin walkway down one wall, just big enough for one person to edge through sideways.

Now they just had to wait.

Flick wandered through into the great hall where preparations for the winners' party were well under way. A team of caterers were busily decorating dozens of tables. Flick could see Winston up on the stage looking at the back of the TV screen. She watched him for a while before returning to the hallway to see if the plan was working. Two men were attempting to carry a large bouquet of flowers in from the courtyard. Cursing and muttering, they were struggling to squeeze past all the equipment cases. It was surely only a matter of time. Gemma sat on one of the cases and picked at her nails, Charlie stared out the door at the view, and Kevin and Saanvi fiddled with some settings on their cameras. After a while Flick started to pace up and down.

And then, finally, it happened.

One of the caterers appeared from the great hall. "You can't leave these here," he complained. "My staff need access."

"We just need to do a bit more filming," said Gemma.

"But do you have to leave your cases like this, blocking the hallway?"

"We need all this equipment. We'll only be about an hour."

"An hour? That's simply not acceptable. I'm going to talk to Mr De Haas."

He stormed off down the hallway and disappeared up the stairs.

Saanvi winked at Flick and got ready. Saanvi placed her camera on her shoulder and Charlie stood in the middle of the hallway, the stairs in the background. They had written him a long script, all about the history of the castle, the party that was being prepared for later, and how the competition was coming to an end now that there were only two teams left. Not that Charlie would need it. Flick knew if there was one thing he could be relied upon to do well, it was talk. Once he started, entire geological periods could pass before he took a breath.

Flick watched the staircase. Within a couple of minutes, she could hear the caterer coming back down the stairs talking to someone. She saw their feet appear as they descended. She watched and waited. Both the people coming down the stairs had two legs. People were so predictable. One set of black trousers, worn by the caterer, and next to him came a set of baggy dark blue silk trousers. These could only belong to Lukas De Haas. No one else would be seen dead in trousers like that.

Flick signalled to Kevin, and before they were spotted by De Haas the two of them slipped out into the courtyard, heading towards their van, which had been deliberately parked in front of the tower entrance. De Haas would be nicely distracted arguing with Gemma right about now, thought Flick, not something she would wish on anyone. Slipping between the side of the van and the castle wall, Flick punched in the pin and opened the tower door. Kevin started filming as they entered and began to climb the stairs.

42
The TV

When they had finished filming, Kevin helped Flick down the stairs and together they slipped back out of the green door into the courtyard.

They opened the van and climbed in. Kevin took out a laptop and swiftly uploaded all the footage they'd captured. He then quickly and efficiently edited it, added the fades and transitions, and finished tidying it all up. Then he pulled out a very small black USB stick from his pocket and plugged it into the laptop.

"This is what Winston says we need for the TV," he explained. "We just need to stick this into one of the slots in the back. It's so small no one will notice it." He held out a little box with buttons. "After the official film has finished, you can use this little remote to change the TV input. When you do that, it'll automatically start playing the film on the USB." He pulled out the stick from the laptop.

Flick took both the stick and the remote.

"Just in case, it might also be worth using this." Kevin handed Flick a little tube of superglue. "To make sure no one can remove it."

"Got it," said Flick. "But I might need your help again in looking official."

"No problem. I'll bring my camera." Kevin grinned, putting it back on his shoulder.

He slid the side of the van shut and they set off across the courtyard towards the main entrance of the castle. When they arrived, they found Saanvi, Gemma and Charlie very slowly packing up the cases.

"All good?" asked Charlie eagerly.

"All done," said Flick. "We got what we needed."

Charlie looked relieved.

"So," Flick said to Gemma, "we just need to check the TV is set up OK in the great hall."

"I'll come and help," she replied.

Flick, Saanvi, Kevin, Charlie and Gemma entered the great hall. The catering staff had nearly finished laying the tables. A group of workmen were setting up glitter cannons on either side of the stage while others were filling a large net with hundreds of red balloons which they were suspending from the ceiling.

Gemma led the way in case they were challenged, but as it was, no one paid them any attention, and they walked uncontested up onto the stage. Flick approached the giant TV hanging on the rear wall. She ran her fingers around the back and was able to ease it forward a few millimetres. She felt for an unused USB slot and pushed the little stick into it. Taking the tube of superglue, she ran it all around the edge of the slot. Now, even if someone found it, they would never be able to pull it out.

"I've got an even better idea," whispered Kevin. He took the tube from her and ran the rest of the glue along the top back edge of the TV and down the sides. "Now no one will even be able to get to the back of the TV."

All four of them pressed the TV as hard as they could against the back wall and held it there for a couple of minutes until the glue had set.

"There's no way that's moving now," said Gemma with satisfaction.

Kevin gently tried and failed to pull the TV forward. "Looks good to me."

They were ready for the show to begin.

43
The Show

Later that evening, Dominic Drake stood on the stage of the great hall and surveyed the scene before him. He had won. All this was for him. The cameras would soon be filming his moment of triumph. All the council members of the Global Order of Magic were sitting on a raised platform at the back of the hall, the champagne was already flowing, and everyone knew the victory was his. The announcement was simply a formality. The Fox had fallen for his trap and opened the deposit box, and it was then a very simple task of framing that stupid one-legged girl with the theft of the painting. With her in prison there was no one else left in the competition apart from his team. The chancellorship was his.

Behind the stage, where there had once been four flags, there was now just one. The one with a silver cane on it. He allowed himself a little smirk. It was ironic that he would soon be declared the winner because of the trick that Harry and Ruby had performed. But in reality, his most magnificent trick was one that no one would ever know about – the way he had played the Fox.

They'd installed confetti cannons on either side of the stage, and hundreds of balloons were ready to drop from a large net attached to the ceiling. All in preparation for the moment when he would be crowned chancellor. The moment when he would have the right to know the method behind the greatest trick ever invented. Even if that wretched girl's father couldn't be found, and even if he never got his hands on the actual Bell System, Drake would be able to demand the method. And with that information, he could build his own. Die Glocke was impressive, but with the full-sized Bell System, by all accounts ... well, absolutely anything was possible.

And then Drake saw Flick, Charlie, the Great Fox and Linth's chief of police walk through the entrance.

For a moment, he stood dead still. He couldn't believe his eyes.

Coming to his senses, Drake made a beeline for the police chief.

"What's this criminal doing here?" he demanded, pointing to Flick.

"We have investigated," Victor calmly replied, "and concluded that she has done nothing wrong."

"Well, that's simply not possible."

"We're the police. Are you telling us you know more than we do?"

"Apparently so."

While Drake continued to argue, Flick, Charlie and the Fox were collected by a crew member and led backstage. Another flag was hastily unfurled next to Drake's silver cane banner – the fox's head.

Drake, however, was not giving up. He stormed backstage to find Christina, who was doing a mic check in the wings.

"You can't let the Fox re-join the competition," Drake protested.

"And why is that?" Christina asked smoothly.

"His team stole from Lukas De Haas's bank."

"Not according to the police. They've now been through all the footage from the vault and there is no evidence the girl stole anything at all. In fact, I've heard that the footage shows Flick opening a deposit box that didn't contain anything. She couldn't have stolen something from an empty box. Now if you will excuse me, I have a finale to present."

"You'll do no such thing," said Drake furiously, attempting to block her way. But Christina just pushed past him calmly and walked onto the stage. She was handed a microphone headset. The spotlights flickered on, and the crew called for silence.

They counted her in, and then she was off.

"What we're about to show you tonight are the final tricks in this nail-biting competition, so prepare to be amazed and bamboozled. First up we have Flick and Charlie and their sensational vault trick. After that we'll be inviting Harry and Ruby onto the stage to introduce their trick."

The large screen above her head lit up and the lights dimmed.

44
The Performance

The Great Fox, black suit, white shirt, no tie, was standing on the roof of the De Haas Bank.

"Good evening. I'm the Great Fox, and tonight we're going to attempt the heist of the century – to make twenty-five million euros' worth of diamonds disappear from one of the most secure vaults in the world."

The camera panned round to show the Linth night sky-line, all lit up, before returning to the Fox.

"I'm standing on the roof of one of the oldest and most secure banks in the world, but tonight all that is going to change."

He walked across the roof, reached some steps and started to descend. The handheld camera moved along ahead of him.

As he walked down the steps, the Fox delivered his lines straight down the lens.

"For the past three hundred years, the De Haas Bank has kept its clients' valuables safe. It has never had a break-in. Until tonight."

The programme cut to shots filmed in the daylight of the Fox with Flick and Charlie standing on a different roof, the bank visible over their shoulders on the opposite side of the street. The camera spun dizzily around them.

The Fox's voice talked over the film. "This is Flick and this is Charlie. They are my apprentices."

The camera then panned out to show a tall man with long dark hair and an elaborate goatee beard who was dressed like a pirate.

"This is Lukas De Haas, owner of the magnificent bank we can see behind us. Mr De Haas, thank you for joining us. Tell us a little about your bank."

The camera zoomed in on Lukas, who nodded and said, "My family has owned it for more than three hundred years. During that time, we have offered private banking and wealth management services to Europe's elite."

The Fox asked, "And is there a vault in the bank?"

"There is. It is deep underground and has a steel-reinforced concrete door over a metre thick operated by a dual-action combination lock. No one has ever breached our security."

"What is the most valuable item in your vault?"

"There are some diamonds that belong to my family. They are worth around twenty-five million euros."

"Mr De Haas, are you a betting man?"

"I enjoy an occasional flutter."

"In that case," the Fox said, "I'm going to make you a wager. I bet that these two children can make those diamonds vanish."

The camera zoomed in on a nervous-looking Charlie and Flick.

"These kids are about as far from experienced bank robbers as you can get, but I'm telling you that they will remove those diamonds from the vault without setting off any of your bank's security measures or damaging the vault itself. I can also tell you that the theft will take place at exactly 9.30 p.m. this Friday, and it will all be captured on film."

The camera cut to Lukas, who laughed and said, "That is a fantasy, I'm afraid. We have an exceptional security team."

"I'm sure you do."

"No one has achieved what you are suggesting in three hundred years. And believe me, plenty have tried."

The camera swung back and showed the Fox shaking hands with De Haas.

"It seems we have a deal, Mr De Haas. Flick and Charlie will do what has never been done before. They will do the impossible."

The next twenty minutes of the film showed footage of

the vault and its security features while the Fox's voice-over explained each detail. The section ended with shots of the diamonds themselves glinting in the bright white lights of the vault.

The film cut to footage of the Fox in the control room. He explained how the CCTV was monitored. He also explained what would happen if it all went wrong. If a robbery was detected the bank would go into lockdown, the vault would be opened and checked, the TV crew's camera would be removed from the vault, and everyone would be forced to leave the premises while the place was made secure. Footage was then shown of the security guards, eyes glued to the screens, each of them wearing a camera headset so the audience could see what they saw. The film played some test footage from these head cameras to check they were working.

The film then jumped to footage recorded just before the trick was due to take place. The Fox had made it down from the roof. He stood in his black suit in the magnificent marble entrance hall of the bank and gazed into the lens of the camera. "The time is now nine twenty-eight," he announced solemnly.

The camera zoomed in on a large clock on the wall behind him.

"Let us now invite Lukas De Haas to join us here in the foyer of his bank."

Lukas appeared through a door next to the cashier stations.

He walked the length of the foyer and stood next to the Fox, and together they watched the clock tick down.

The Fox said, "You have three security guards on duty in the control room?"

"That is correct."

"And they are constantly watching the CCTV feed?"

"They are."

"And they know that the theft is about to take place?"

"They do. We are ready."

The clock ticked onwards to nine thirty.

"That's it," announced the Fox. "The diamonds have been stolen. We would now like you to check. Can we ask your security team to open the vault?"

45
The Reveal

De Haas spoke into a radio. "Open the vault."

Suddenly an alarm bell rang out, deafeningly loud.

Lukas glanced at the Fox and raised an eyebrow.

The Fox looked worried. He said something unintelligible over the din of the alarm. In the background, the shutters in front of the cashier stations were automatically closing.

The alarm continued to ring loudly. In the back of the shot, a guard could be seen rushing into the foyer. He approached the Fox and De Haas and started to usher them out.

The camera went wobbly as it was carried through the doors and out into the street, still filming Lukas and the Fox.

Once outside and steady again, it focused on the Fox, who looked flustered as he said, "Something's obviously gone wrong. I hope Flick and Charlie are OK."

The programme cut to a live feed of the CCTV, and then to the headcams of the security guards. Two of them had left the control room and were entering the lift. When they reached the basement, they exited into the service corridor and ran to the vault door. Here they both typed in their security numbers to open it. They eased the heavy door back on its hinges and the lights flickered on inside.

One of them stepped into the vault. He picked up the camera and tripod and took it to the door where he passed it to the other guard. Then he began to check the walls and safety deposit boxes while the other guard carried the camera and tripod down the corridor and into the lift. He pressed G as the doors closed.

The film then reverted to footage from the headset of the guard still in the vault. He was slowly and methodically scanning the room.

It then cut back to the Fox and Lukas, who were still outside the bank.

The Fox asked Lukas, "Can you ask your guard in the vault if there is any sign of a break-in?"

De Haas muttered into the radio. He listened briefly, then replied that the guard had reported nothing suspicious.

The Fox said, "Can you ask the guard to check the diamonds?"

The headset camera showed the guard walking over to the glass table. He opened the black box. It contained just one object. A playing card with the silhouette of a fox's head on it.

"The diamonds appear to have gone," said the Fox. "Can you confirm?"

Lukas spoke into his radio again and listened to the response. "They've gone," he said. He slowly lowered the radio from his ear and stared at the Fox wide-eyed.

"What's the time?" the Fox asked.

Lukas said, "Nine thirty-four."

"It looks as if Flick and Charlie carried out the theft right on time. But where are they? Can you ask the guard to walk all around the vault so we can see how they got in?"

Yet again the film cut back to footage from the vault. The images were jumpy, but the vault looked to be completely undamaged. Nothing appeared out of place.

Now a member of the TV crew in a baseball cap could be seen approaching the Fox and whispering something to him. The Fox listened, and then announced to the camera, "I'm just asking if anyone knows where Flick and Charlie are."

The Fox looked away from the camera towards the crew member, who was now out of shot, and nodded, saying, "Yes, I think we've found them."

The camera angle shifted and panned out to show both the Fox and Lukas. The Fox had his arm round Lukas's shoulder. "The diamonds have been stolen without your vault being damaged or anything showing up on your CCTV. How is that possible?"

Lukas laughed ruefully. "That is a good question. And one I shall be sure to ask my security team."

The Fox, with his arm still round Lukas, slowly turned him through ninety degrees so that his back was now to the bank.

Standing on the other side of the street, lit up by a spotlight, were Flick and Charlie.

"There they are. And they look absolutely fine."

Flick and Charlie waved as the camera zoomed in.

The camera then switched back to the Fox, who stepped away from Lukas and asked, "But where are the diamonds?"

The camera panned around the two of them.

"Check your waistcoat pocket, Mr De Haas."

Frowning, Lukas reached inside his waistcoat and brought out a black box.

He burst into shocked laughter. "How did that get there?"

He opened the box, and the diamonds could be seen gleaming in the light.

46
The Final Film

When the film ended, Flick and Charlie stood on the stage and accepted the thunderous applause. They both bowed. Several members of the Global Order leapt to their feet to give them a standing ovation.

Flick reached into her pocket and took out the little remote. She pressed play and a new film started.

Christina turned towards the screen in surprise. "Oh, is there more? I wasn't expecting that."

She held up her hands and the great hall fell quiet.

The new footage showed Charlie standing in the castle hallway. He explained how the De Haas family had made its money. During the Second World War, they had been more than happy to look after stolen valuables for high-ranking Nazis. It was terribly good for business. After the war, many of these deposit boxes remained crammed with gold and priceless works of art. The De Haas family made no effort to return them to their rightful owners but instead borrowed against the value of these items. This enabled them to expand their business and open more banks. They became millionaires as a result.

Next the film cut to Flick detailing Lukas De Haas's plan to bribe the members of the Global Order of Magic with some of these stolen treasures.

"Wait a minute!" bellowed De Haas from the audience. "Don't believe these lies!" He frantically tried to push his way towards the stage as the film continued to play.

On-screen, the film cut to footage of Flick in De Haas's office in the tower. She removed the painting of the castle from the wall to reveal the location of the safe.

"I'm pretty sure this is where the stolen painting is," Flick could be heard saying before covering the safe back up again.

"Turn this off," ordered Lukas, rushing onto the stage and lunging at Flick and Charlie. "I demand as the owner of this castle that you turn this off at once!" he raged.

Flick and Charlie backed away.

Lukas glared at Christina. "Who is responsible for this?" he demanded.

Christina said nothing, just pressed one finger to her headset as if waiting for instructions.

On the screen, the film cut to footage from the vault showing the deposit box was empty when Flick opened it, proving the painting had already been taken when she got there.

Enraged, De Haas approached the giant screen mounted on the back wall. He tried to pull it forward off its bracket, but it wouldn't budge.

"TURN THIS OFF!" he bellowed.

Unable to move the TV, he rushed to the side of the stage and came back with a fire extinguisher. Wielding it like a battering ram, he hit the screen repeatedly until the glass cracked. The audience watched in shocked silence. It took him several minutes to silence the film, and when he had finished, the television hung on the wall at a drunken angle. The screen was smashed and silent and there was a strong burning smell.

Victor Odermatt stood at the back of the room in stunned silence. Then he raised his phone to his ear and said, "Leo, we need to get into that office and open the safe. I want the whole tower sealed off immediately. No one is to touch a thing."

47
The Trap

De Haas stood in front of the screen, breathing heavily. Then he looked towards the back of the great hall and snarled, "Lock the door."

No one moved. Everyone sat in stunned silence.

"I said LOCK THE DOOR!"

Four large security guards appeared from the hallway. They locked the door and stood in front of it for good measure.

"Did you think," De Haas snarled, glaring at Flick, "that you were the only one with another trick up your sleeve?"

As he said this, the hundreds of red balloons dropped from the ceiling. The audience looked confused. Was this part of the show? Several of them caught balloons and some laughed but Flick wasn't distracted. Her eyes were fixed on the ceiling. Where the net had fallen away it revealed a large black metal bell-shaped object suspended inside a metal frame. It was hanging on a chain from the ceiling.

"What do you think you're doing?" Christina said. She still held her finger to her ear.

But it wasn't De Haas who answered. Instead, Drake stepped forward and smirked. "Don't worry. Soon you won't remember a thing. That little film will be long forgotten." He glanced towards the raised seating at the back where the members of the Global Order were sitting. "Those of you with goggles, put them on and join us in our little demonstration. *You* will remember what you're about to see for the rest of your lives."

Flick saw some of the Global Order putting on dark goggles and ear defenders. The other members looked confused.

"For the rest of you, remembering might become a little tricky," Drake laughed as he tossed De Haas some goggles and ear protectors before producing second pairs for himself. They both quickly put them on and then De Haas took out the large remote control from his waistcoat and started turning some dials.

Die Glocke was already starting to spin.

Flick and Charlie backed away across the stage.

"We've got to go," urged Flick, tugging at Charlie's arm. "Don't look at it."

They made their way to the edge of the stage and down the steps as fast as they could, Charlie holding Flick's hand. They could hear the metal bell spinning faster and faster, making a noise like a jet engine.

The audience looked up, transfixed. Some were still smiling uncertainly. Was this part of the show?

Flick and Charlie ran down the aisle. As the Bell reached full speed it started to emit that familiar rhythmic deep bass tone that Flick could feel inside her – like a heartbeat. She stopped running and looked down at her feet, unable to move. She found herself turning towards the stage. She couldn't stop herself. She was aware of everyone else in the audience slowly getting to their feet.

Suspended above them, Die Glocke began to flash like a strobe light with sparks of electricity and lightning arcing out from it. It fizzled and crackled. Flick clenched her teeth and with all her might tried to lift her left arm to shield her eyes, but it would not budge. It was glued to her side.

The intensity of the flashes increased until Flick's vision started to strobe.

The room went black.

Then blinding white.

Then black.

Then white.

Black then white, faster and faster. On, off, on, off, as the jet engine sound got louder and louder until it became a scream, and then a whistle, its pitch getting higher and higher, turning the room white with noise.

And then everything was silent.

Flick was alone in an infinite white space. It was hard to judge distances because the white stretched out before her on all sides. It had no features. She could feel the terror rising within her. Her breathing became quick and shallow. She swallowed and tried to focus. The floor was solid under her, so she took a step forward and stopped. Something felt different. She looked down. Her prosthetic had gone. She'd got her right leg back. She bent it at the knee, flexed it, took some steps forward, and then jumped up and down on it. It was real. It worked.

She walked forward into the white. Slowly she became aware of voices, echoing and distant. It was impossible to tell where they were coming from. Were they behind her? She turned round. At first she couldn't see; the white of the landscape was too bright. She shielded her eyes.

And then she could hear a different noise. A dog barking. Getting louder and louder. It was Lukas's dog, Nero. He was running across the white towards her. Growling and foaming at the mouth.

He was coming for her.

48
The Whiteness

Flick turned and fled across the white landscape. Despite her terror, it felt amazing to have her leg back. She stretched it out, running faster than she had ever run, but even like this, she knew she could never outrun Nero. His growl was behind her, getting closer.

And then she looked up, and all of a sudden she was in Linth. She could see the cobbled streets and ancient buildings. It was recognizably Linth, except everything was white, as if the colour had been leached from the landscape. She was running up the hill towards the castle, through the narrow streets. There were the familiar shopfronts, but they were all pale as if made of snow. She puffed away, trying to get up the hill. As she ran, she could hear a muffled voice. It sounded like Charlie, but she couldn't tell where it was coming from.

The whiteness grew thicker as if she was suddenly in the midst of deep fog. Now there was nothing around her at all. She kept moving forward. At times, the white drifted past her like clouds, and she occasionally caught a glimpse of the streets as they parted. Now she could only walk on uphill.

And then, just for a moment, the fog cleared, and she found herself in a very narrow street. On the pavement was a bench, and on the bench sat Charlie. He was on his own, head down, rendered in monochrome as if he'd stepped out of a black and white film.

When he saw Flick approaching, he looked up and beamed, running to meet her. They hugged.

"I'm so glad to see you," he said. "Where are we?"

Flick shrugged.

"Is all this made by Die Glocke?" he asked.

"I think this is all in our heads, somehow. Die Glocke affects the mind; that's what the noise and the light do. It's like a dream. Except somehow we're sharing it."

"It's a pretty weird dream. I prefer the one where I'm flying or the one where I'm performing an amazing trick onstage and the audience is loving the fact that—"

"Shh," hissed Flick. "I thought I heard..."

There was the unmistakable sound of footsteps on the cobbles, coming their way.

"In here." Charlie urgently pointed to a doorway on their

left and they tucked themselves in, watching as a figure came out of the mist. Despite the poor visibility, they recognized the Fox immediately. He walked past them and down the street.

"Where's he going?" Charlie whispered.

"Only one way to find out," said Flick.

They stepped out of their doorway and followed him at a safe distance, just able to make him out through the dense cloud. As they came to a crossroads, they paused. Which way had he gone? They peered left, then right, then straight ahead, trying to see through the fog. The mist parted fractionally, and Flick saw the Fox turning right into a narrow alley.

Flick and Charlie turned in after him. The alley felt very cramped with rough stone walls that disappeared into the mist above them, in front of them, and behind them. As the fog parted again, Flick saw the Fox was now with someone else. She recognized his shape immediately – the way he walked, the way he moved his head.

"He's with my dad," she said, increasing her speed.

"Are you sure?" asked Charlie. "I can only see the Fox."

The mist thickened once more, and now they could see about a metre ahead of them. Flick broke into a jog and Charlie ran along beside her. What was her dad doing here?

The alley became narrower still until their shoulders were brushing the stonework on either side. Occasionally the mist would part just enough to see the Fox ahead of them. He was definitely on his own now; there was no sign of her father.

Had Flick imagined him? The alley came to a stop, ending in a set of stairs leading steeply downwards. They started to descend and realized that the steps curved around into a spiral staircase. Down they went. The whiteness cleared, and when Flick peered down into the stairwell, she could see the Fox still descending below her.

And then she heard a faint throbbing sound and felt a deep pulsing in her bones. It was the sound and vibration of the spinning Bell, and it was coming from below, getting louder and louder. They kept going down and down, round and round, heading deeper and deeper underground. As they did, the heartbeat got stronger and stronger, and then with the thumping came a pulsing flash, faint at first and then brighter and brighter, emanating from the bottom of the stairwell. They pressed forward, getting closer and closer to the source. Flashes of lightning shot past them up the centre of the stairwell.

Finally, they arrived at the bottom. They found themselves in a large circular space with a stone floor and walls. It was open above them like a huge chimney, the stairs running around the edge, and in the middle of the floor was the Bell, glowing red hot and spinning, occasional arcs of lightning coming from it and striking the stonework. Flick and Charlie could feel the deep noise pulsing in waves. It reverberated in their ears and chests and minds.

In front of them was the Fox. He was slowly walking towards Die Glocke, hands outstretched as if trying to touch it.

Then they felt a wind. Gentle at first, it became stronger and stronger until the Fox had to lean into it to walk towards the Bell. Still the intensity of it increased. His suit was flapping madly. Flick could feel it pushing her eyes back into her head. And then it tore the Fox's mask off. It flew up the stairwell and disappeared. Still the Fox kept trying to press forward.

Surely he would be killed. Flick managed to grab hold of his arm and tried to pull him back. It was like battling a hurricane.

It was only when Flick touched his arm that the Fox became aware that he was not alone. He shouted something but Flick couldn't make it out above the noise. He tried to push her away, but Charlie joined Flick and they both kept pulling him back. The Fox was mouthing something over and over again. Flick watched his lips.

"It's beautiful," he was saying.

And then there was a new sound. A terrible tearing as the ground below Die Glocke started to split. A large crack opened in front of them as fissures spread out from the centre. The pulses grew in volume, and the Bell started to wobble, becoming unstable. The ground cracked open further. Stone and masonry were falling from above.

The Fox pushed forward one more time, and as he did so the stones beneath him split and he fell into the hole. He screamed and grabbed at the side, hanging from the edge, his legs dangling in the void.

Beneath him was a black bottomless pit.

49
The Bell System

Flick fell to her knees and crawled to the edge, stretching out with her hand to try to grab the Fox. But as she looked down, she was surprised to see her dad, hanging on to a lower ledge. He was shouting and reaching out towards her. As Flick watched her father, the Fox grabbed her hand.

"Flick! Flick!" he shouted.

Flick looked at the Fox. She would need to let go of the Fox to save her dad. The Fox had hold of her hand tightly, trying to pull himself up. Flick was frozen in indecision. Should she let go of the Fox and reach for her father? Was he real? Was any of this real?

"HEEEEEELP!" the Fox screamed up at her.

Flick came to a decision. She took the Fox's hand in both of hers and pulled with all her strength. Charlie appeared at her side and caught hold of the Fox's other hand, and slowly they pulled him out of the hole. As he finally crawled to safety, Flick looked over at the second ledge, but her father had gone.

If he had ever been there.

With stonework falling and crumbling all around them, the three of them ran for the stairs and started to climb. They climbed higher and higher, but the wind in the centre of the stairwell was now a vortex, tearing at their clothes, while Die Glocke wobbled and flashed and pulsed below them. They pushed upwards, each step nearer safety, huge chunks of stone falling past them into the black hole below.

Then the stairs started to disintegrate under their feet. The stone became whiter, the fog descended, and Flick found herself alone once more. All was quiet and she was back on an infinite plane of white.

Slowly the wisps of mist blew away as if on a gentle breeze.

Flick was back in the great hall, looking at the stage. Charlie was by her side, eyes closed, rooted to the spot, and they were surrounded by the audience, who were also standing motionless. She could see the Fox fighting with Drake and De Haas on the stage.

"Flick! Flick!" the Fox shouted.

On the right side of the platform was a metal ladder that led up to the lighting gantry. The Fox was trying to climb it to get to the Bell, and Drake and De Haas were trying to stop him. The Fox had got partway up the ladder, but Drake had hold of his right leg. De Haas reached out and grabbed his left leg. He yanked hard and the Fox fell backwards off the ladder, landing on top of Drake and De Haas, arms and legs flailing as they all hit the ground. Then the Fox was on his feet again, calling out her name repeatedly and trying to climb back up the ladder. His mask had been pulled off but this time he climbed faster than Drake or De Haas could react, and he was soon out of their reach.

"Flick!" the Fox shouted again. "WAKE UP!"

There was still mist around the periphery of Flick's vision, but she could see him climbing higher and higher until he reached a gantry that ran across the ceiling towards Die Glocke. Flick expected Drake and De Haas to try to follow, but instead De Haas ran to the side of the stage and pulled some levers. The Fox's gantry lurched away and swung to the back of the stage. The Fox could no longer reach the Bell.

Flick understood what the Fox was trying to do. Get to Die Glocke and disable it. Stop the power it had over them. She looked around. On the left side of the auditorium was another ladder. She tried to trace where it led but another wave of white fog swept over her, preventing her from seeing. She waited a beat for the fog to clear. It didn't.

She had to act.

She ran through the white clouds of fog in the direction of the ladder. It loomed out of the mist, and she started to climb. Up she went, waves of white all around her. She got to the top and stepped onto a gantry that stretched out before her. As far as she could tell it was going in the right direction, towards the Bell.

Up here, the noise was deafening. She put her hands over her ears and stepped forward. She couldn't see anything at all now.

"Take three steps forward and then stop."

It was the muffled voice of the Fox. Could he see her from the parallel gantry?

"Three steps and then stop," the Fox repeated.

Flick took just three steps blindly into the white and then stopped.

"Now turn ninety degrees to your right and take another three steps."

Turn to her right? She thought the gantry ran straight across the ceiling. If she turned to her right and stepped off, it was a long fall.

"Are you sure?" she called.

"Yes. Ninety degrees to your right and then another three steps."

She turned ninety degrees to the right and paused, taking a deep breath and closing her eyes. The visibility was so bad it didn't make much difference anyway.

Then she stepped out.

She was relieved to feel solid metal under her foot. She took the three steps.

"Now ninety degrees left and take five steps," said the distant voice of the Fox.

She followed his directions.

"The chain is on your left."

She opened her eyes and looked to her left. The white cleared for a fraction of a second and she could see it. If she leant forward, it would be within reach. She put out her hand and touched it, and as the white cleared a little more, she could see the top link was on a metal hook attached to the ceiling. She grabbed the chain with both hands and pulled it towards her. The top link edged along the hook. It was very heavy, but she kept pulling, and by leaning back with all her weight it slowly came off.

And then it fell.

Flick toppled backwards into the fog as the weight came away. Panic rose inside her. Was she falling? Then she smacked into the hard metal gantry, hitting her head and yelping in pain. Relief washed over her.

There was an almighty crash.

The fog vanished and Flick could see the Bell had smashed through the wooden floor of the stage below.

A huge spark of electricity flew into the air and there was a bang like a thunderclap. As Flick looked down, she could see the Fox on the stage. He'd climbed down from his gantry and was hitting Die Glocke with a fire extinguisher. The Bell was badly damaged. It was still spinning, but it had slowed and the noise was diminished. The Fox kept hitting it again and again and again.

As her surroundings returned, Flick could see the stage and the audience in more detail. She slowly got to her feet and stood, looking down. She watched as De Haas grabbed the Fox's arm, pulling him away from the Bell. The Fox fought back and the two of them wrestled.

The Fox needed her help. Glancing around, Flick noticed another chain attached to the gantry. She unhooked one end and held it in her right hand. Then she climbed over the edge and sat on the rail, holding on to the chain with both hands. She looked at the stage. It was a long way down. If this went wrong, it would hurt. A lot.

She let herself fall forward, swinging out on the chain. She flew through the air towards the Bell and the stage. As she reached the platform she let go, hitting the wooden boards with a thud, making sure she fell on the side of her good leg, and then sliding along. She came to a stop next to the Bell and stumbled to her feet.

Lying in the wreckage of the wooden stage, the Bell was still spinning and pulsing out light but much more slowly now. Beyond the Bell she could see that Drake had also piled into the Fox, pushing him back, away from the Bell, and knocking him to the ground. As the Fox fell, he looked up at Flick and threw the extinguisher towards her. Flick watched it fly, arcing high into the air above Drake and De Haas and over the top of the Bell. Because of the flashing strobe effect still coming from the Bell, the image came towards her in jerks. She reached up and tried to catch it, but the weight of it slammed into her hands and tore itself free, falling to the floor.

She bent and picked it up. When she had steadied herself, she could see that Drake and De Haas were standing over the Fox. Nero appeared from the side of the stage and leapt on top of him. But the Fox wasn't looking at any of them. He was staring past Nero, past De Haas, past Drake, and past the Bell. Looking at her. Their eyes met as he silently communicated with her.

She knew what she had to do.

She angled the extinguisher in her hands so that the full force of her swing would hit the Bell from the side, and then she brought it down from above her head against it. The Bell toppled over and skidded across the stage, sparks flying as it smashed against the back wall.

The noise and flashing ceased.

It stopped spinning.

It lay there, crackling and smouldering.

Drake and De Haas looked at it open-mouthed.

There was a loud banging from the back of the hall followed by shouts of "Police!", and then there was a crash as the door was smashed off its hinges and dozens of officers swarmed in and stormed the stage.

"Arrest them both," Victor shouted, running onto the stage behind them.

The audience, released from the power of the Bell, stood around bewildered. Some sat down in shock, and a few were crying with the trauma.

Flick ran to the Fox and tried to pull Nero back by his collar, hoping to get him off. She pulled but the Doberman was too heavy to budge. She pulled and pulled, but his jaws were latched on to the Fox's arm and wouldn't let go. And then there were arms around Flick pulling her back as two police officers came to her rescue. One fired a dart into Nero's neck and the dog went limp. A couple of medics rushed over.

The Fox was moving now. He was reaching out to her.

"You OK?" he asked.

Flick nodded. "Thank you," she whispered, taking his hand.

The Fox nodded and gave her a weak smile as he was gently lifted onto a stretcher and carried off by the medics. Flick walked by his side, still holding his hand until he was slowly lowered from the stage, and she had to let go. She then watched as he was wheeled across the great hall, her eyes following him all the way until he passed through the door and out of sight.

Charlie, back to his senses, came and put his arm around her, and she hugged him back. They stared out across the great hall for a while and then she noticed his head was turned. Flick followed his gaze. The wreckage of Die Glocke lay in several shattered pieces half embedded in the back wall of the stage, glowing red hot and smouldering. The extinguisher was lying across it. The two of them stood in silence. Even Charlie seemed to have run out of words. With their arms still around each other they turned back towards the great hall and watched De Haas and Drake being led away in handcuffs.

50
The Chancellor

Following their arrests, Dominic Drake and Lukas De Haas were both expelled from the Global Order of Magic. The Great Fox, as the new chancellor, was saddened at De Haas's betrayal and vowed to make sure that neither of them would ever be allowed to join again. Harry and Ruby confessed to cheating in their final trick – it turned out that the audience member they had chosen was in on it. How original.

In the days following, the police investigated the contents of the vault, the painting was recovered from the safe in the tower, and De Haas was charged with theft. Because of the danger posed by the plans on the back of the painting it was destroyed. The rest of the loot was also recovered from the deposit boxes in the bank, the living relatives were traced, and the items finally returned to their rightful families. De Haas had stolen from his own bank and was struck off from all banking institutions and barred from owning, running or even working in a bank ever again. This caused a huge drop in confidence in the Linth bank, of course, and with all the negative publicity, many people withdrew their money, causing it to go bust.

Not a bad outcome, thought Flick.

51

The Applause

The Great Fox bounded onto the stage to rapturous applause. The screen behind him swirled with the fox's head logo while high energy music with a thumping bass played from the speakers.

"Ladies and gentlemen," Christina shouted, trying to be heard above the din, "I give you the new chancellor of the Global Order of Magic: THE GREAT FOX!"

Fireworks shot up from either side of the stage as the Fox spun round with his arms out and performed a series of elaborate bows.

Flick and Charlie watched from behind some black curtains at the side of the stage, waiting to come on.

"He's an idiot, isn't he?" said Charlie. "I mean, what kind of man spends his whole life wearing a fox's mask?"

"I don't think he can ever eat in public because of it," said Flick.

"That's dedication to his act. But it's also fairly crazy."

"Yes, but you were right about him. We could trust him. Thank you."

"I guess we're all strange, just in different ways," said Charlie.

They heard a cough and turned around. Victor was standing there grinning from ear to ear.

"Congratulations," he said.

Flick realized it was the first time she had seen the chief of police smile.

"I've just found out that the Fox didn't explain everything to you," he said.

"What's that?" asked Charlie.

"Just after I released you, the Fox showed me the whole film from the vault. He worked out that De Haas and Drake were going to try and frame you, so that's why he made sure you filmed the empty deposit box."

"So I'm free to go?" asked Flick.

"More than that! You're the hero of the hour. You uncovered what was really going on."

He reached out and shook Flick's hand. "You have done this town a great service," he said warmly. "You exposed what De Haas was up to. Thank you."

He waved goodbye and disappeared down a set of

steps just as Harry came up them. When he saw Flick and Charlie, he hesitated, looking extremely uncomfortable, and started to turn away. But then he stopped himself. He finally seemed to reach a decision and turned to face them.

"Look," he said. "I'm about to leave Linth, but I wanted to say ... I never knew the bank was run on things stolen by the Nazis and that they were using it to bribe the council and ... I'm sorry. If I'd known about De Haas, I would never have agreed to help him and Drake."

"I don't think anyone knew," said Charlie kindly.

"Well, you managed to work it out," said Harry.

"They lied to you and manipulated you," said Flick. "That's just the kind of people they are."

Harry reached out his hand and Charlie shook it. Then he turned to Flick. Instead of taking Harry's hand, Flick stepped forward and hugged him, surprising herself in the process. "Thank you for saying sorry," she said gruffly.

"All the best," mumbled Harry, awkwardly untangling himself from Flick. He turned and walked away.

Flick and Charlie faced the stage just in time to hear Christina say, "And now please put your hands together for the two stars of the show – FLICK AND CHARLIE!"

Charlie smiled at Flick and the two of them stepped out onto the stage.

52
The Flight

Flick and Charlie were on the Great Fox's private plane – the black Gulfstream with the cream leather interior. They had plonked themselves in the comfy seats at the back, while the Fox sat opposite them next to Ursula, the freshly retired chancellor of the Global Order of Magic. She was still wearing her purple cape.

"I promise you we will now go and meet your father," said the Fox, readjusting his damaged arm in its sling.

"I've heard that before," said Flick.

"I know. This time it's certain. I'm sorry I didn't trust you enough to explain everything to you. That was wrong of me. And I need to thank you properly for your brilliance with the film. Thanks to you, De Haas is in prison, and the stolen valuables have been returned to their rightful owners."

"To be fair, Charlie did most of the hard work on that. He even managed to talk to Saanvi."

Charlie looked very pleased with himself.

"I think," said Ursula, "that you should *all* be congratulated. You managed to plan a trick that won the competition and kept the Bell System out of the hands of Drake and De Haas. Not bad for a few days' work."

The Fox gave a little bow in his seat and Flick beamed with pride.

"And you even managed to find the time to work out that Harry and Ruby cheated in their final trick."

The Fox turned to Flick. "I'm sorry I didn't explain the finer details of the trick to you."

"Finer details?" said Flick. "You didn't explain *anything* to me!"

"I thought that Drake and De Haas might use Die Glocke on you, so I couldn't risk you knowing that I suspected De Haas had already stolen the painting, and I couldn't explain the details of my plan to prove the deposit box was empty. I knew that if they used it on you, they would find out everything and beat us, but if you only knew part of the plan, I would be able to fool them."

Flick scowled at the Fox. "So, you were quite happy for me to be exposed to Die Glocke, as long as I didn't reveal all your plans?"

The Fox stared impassively back at her from behind his mask.

"When did you start to suspect De Haas was working with Drake?" asked Charlie.

"From the moment we arrived I started to have my doubts about him," explained the Fox, "and I needed to change my plans to cover that possible betrayal. I just couldn't risk explaining it all to you. I've spent my whole life keeping secrets and I'm not very good at trusting others." He shrugged apologetically.

Flick shook her head. "No, you're not very good at trusting others. And what about that video showing my dad disappearing and the note in the lorry?"

"The very fact that you're asking me tells me you know the answer."

"All made up by you?"

"Yes," nodded the Fox. "The video was of a crew member who I hoped was about the same height and build as your dad, and with the terrible quality of the film I sent it to Gemma and hoped I would get away with it. The note was also written by me."

"Well, that explains why it didn't say very much," mused Charlie.

"You were very disappointed that your dad wasn't here," continued the Fox. "I couldn't risk you leaving, and that was the best way I could think to make you want to stay."

"And you thought lying about my dad again would help with my disappointment?"

"I promise I will be more honest with you from now on."

And there it was. The promise of a magician who had fooled her again.

As the plane took off, Flick looked at Charlie with his headphones on and eyes closed, listening to music. Then she turned her head and watched the Fox. He was gazing out of the window, his mask still on, hiding his face, his thoughts, his feelings.

Magicians make you doubt. It's what they do for a living; it's the essence of who they are. Did he mean what he said? Would he take her to her dad? Only time would tell. In the meantime, she would listen to Charlie. He was right. She needed to appreciate the other people in her life rather than spend all her time worrying about her dad.

So, as the plane climbed, she pushed her worries out of her mind and did just that. She called her mum and told her she loved her. Then she told her all about ... well, everything. When she'd finished, she looked out of the window and thought she might just be ready for whatever came next. As the plane banked, she was pressed back into her seat. She drank in the bright blue sky, beautiful sunshine and white fluffy clouds. Then she smiled and closed her eyes.

53
The Question

In case you're wondering, we stole the diamonds from the vault that couldn't be opened, while watched by security guards and buried deep under one of the most secure banks in Europe ... very easily. I've told you how a lot of it was done but see if you can work the rest of it out. Like all good tricks, the method was simple but effective. I'm sure it won't take you long to figure it out, and when you do, send me a message, because you might be able to help us on our next assignment. What comes next is truly terrifying and we'll definitely need someone with your skills to help us.

54
The Answer

A TV.

On the TV a film started to play, showing footage from cameras attached to Flick and Charlie. Their starting position for the trick was inside a Channel Seven van parked near the front of the bank, and the time stamp in the bottom corner showed 9.00 p.m. The Fox had taken up his position in the foyer and his conversation with De Haas could be heard over the shots of Flick and Charlie putting on black overalls so they looked like TV crew. They both put on baseball caps, pulling them down low over their eyes, and then they left the van to move to their next position.

Entering the bank, they walked across the foyer, out of shot of the cameras filming the Fox, and through the door at the side of the cashier stations and into the back corridor. They stopped near the lift and waited.

The audio from the foyer of the Fox talking could be heard.

"The time is now nine twenty-eight. Let us now invite Lukas De Haas to join us here in the foyer of his bank."

There was a pause as De Haas arrived and then the Fox continued. "You have three security guards on duty in the control room?"

"That is correct," said De Haas.

"And they are constantly watching the CCTV feed?"

"They are."

"And they know that the theft is about to take place?"

"They do. We are ready."

The film cut to shots from the previous night. It explained that yesterday evening while setting up the vault camera, a heavily disguised Flick switched the black box containing the diamonds with another, identical black box, which she left in the centre of the glass table. This box didn't contain any diamonds. Instead, it held a heat generator – a clever electrical device with a timer that had been set by Charlie. At exactly 9.29 p.m. this box started to get very hot, and within a couple of minutes, it produced enough heat that the vault's sensors detected it and then sounded the alarm. Flick placed the box containing the diamonds in a hidden slot in the back of the vault camera.

The film cut back to Flick and Charlie standing in the back corridor of the bank where they were waiting near the lift. The time stamp in the bottom corner showed 9.32 p.m. and the alarm could be heard going off. It was very loud.

Immediately two guards left the control room and ran past Flick and Charlie towards the lift.

The audio from the foyer was played over the top of these shots.

The Fox said, "Something's obviously gone wrong. I hope Flick and Charlie are OK."

The film cut to the headset cameras on the security guards as they entered the lift. When they reached the basement, they burst out into the service corridor and ran to the vault door, where they typed in their pin numbers to open it. They eased the door back on its hinges and the lights flickered on inside.

One of them stepped into the vault. He picked up the camera and tripod and took it to the door where he passed it to the other guard. Then he began to check the walls and safety deposit boxes while the other guard carried the camera and tripod down the corridor and into the lift. He pressed G as the doors closed.

The film returned to footage from the headset of the guard in the vault. He was scanning the room.

The film cut back to the Fox and Lukas, now outside the bank.

The Fox asked Lukas, "Can you ask your guard in the vault if there is any sign of a break-in?"

De Haas spoke into the radio.

Eventually the guard reported that he could see nothing suspicious.

The Fox said, "Can you ask the guard to check the diamonds?"

The footage from the guard's headset camera as he walked over to the glass table showed him opening the black box. It contained a playing card with a silhouette of a fox's head on it.

There were no diamonds.

"The diamonds appear to have gone," said the Fox. "Can you confirm?"

Lukas spoke into his radio again and listened to the response. "They've gone," he said.

The Fox looked at De Haas. "What's the time?"

Lukas said, "Nine thirty-four."

The Fox said, "It looks as if Flick and Charlie carried out the theft right on time. But where are they? Can you ask the guard to walk all around the vault so we can see how they got in?"

The film cut to footage from the guard's head-mounted camera. The footage was jumpy, but the vault looked to be completely undamaged. Nothing appeared out of place.

The film cut back to Flick and Charlie standing in the back corridor. They were watching the light showing the lift was ascending. The security guard was bringing the camera up. Bringing it to Flick and Charlie.

Flick met the guard carrying the camera as the lift doors opened, keeping her cap low so he didn't see her face. He was in a rush to get back down to the vault, so he barely looked at her. Flick and Charlie took the camera down the corridor, out through the security doors and into the foyer.

The TV crew in the foyer were also being ejected and Flick and Charlie joined them.

Once outside, they made their way past the chaos of the production team moving their equipment out of the foyer and, still carrying the camera, walked around the side of the building.

Flick put the camera down and removed the diamonds from the slot at the back. With them in her hand, she walked round to the front of the bank.

The camera cut to a member of the TV crew wearing a baseball cap approaching the Fox. As the camera zoomed in, it became obvious that it was Flick. As Flick leant in to talk to the Fox, she pressed the diamonds into his left hand, the move shielded from the cameras by the angle of her body. Flick stepped away and the Fox walked back to De Haas and said to the camera, "I'm just asking if anyone knows where Flick and Charlie are."

The camera zoomed in on the Fox.

The Fox looked back at the member of his crew, who was now out of shot, and nodded, saying, "Yes, I think we've found them."

The angle shifted and panned out to show the Fox and Lukas. The Fox walked over to Lukas and put his arm round his shoulder and said, "The diamonds have been stolen without your vault being damaged or anything showing up on your CCTV. How is that possible?"

Lukas laughed ruefully. "That is a good question. And one I shall be sure to ask my security team."

The Fox, with his arm still around Lukas, slowly turned him through ninety degrees so that his back was now to the bank.

The same shot was shown again in slow motion. At this speed you could see that while the Fox was turning De Haas around, his hand with the diamonds in it slipped inside De Haas's waistcoat for a split second.

Standing on the other side of the street, lit up by a spotlight, were Flick and Charlie.

The Fox said, "There they are. And they look absolutely fine."

The camera zoomed in on Flick and Charlie and they waved.

The camera switched back to the Fox, who stepped away from Lukas and said, "But where are the diamonds?"

The camera panned around the two of them.

The Fox said, "Check your waistcoat pocket, Mr De Haas."

Lukas reached inside his waistcoat and brought out the black box.

He burst into shocked laughter. "How did that get there?"

He opened the box, and the diamonds could be seen gleaming in the light.

THE FOX FILES

A step-by-step guide to performing an amazing card trick

This one is easy to learn, but very impressive!

1. Make sure you have a complete set of 52 cards (remove the jokers and advertising cards from the pack).

2. Give the pack to your audience member. You're going to get them to perform this trick!

3. Ask them to shuffle the cards.

4. Ask them to deal themselves nine cards and then select one of the nine (but make sure *you* don't see it).

THIS IS THE <u>CHOSEN</u> CARD. YOUR AUDIENCE MEMBER SHOULD REMEMBER <u>it</u>!

5. Ask them to put their selected card on top of the other eight cards. They should then give the rest of the pack another good shuffle and put it on top of the nine cards.

6. Now ask them to deal out four piles of cards, one pile at a time, face up. As they deal the cards, they are to count backwards from ten. If the number they say matches the value on the card they are to stop dealing that pile.

TEN

NINE-STOP COUNTING!

For example, if they say 'seven' and deal the number seven at the same time, they should then stop that pile and start a new one. If they count all the way back to one and they haven't matched the value, ask them to cap the pile with the next card placed face down. That pile will end up with eleven cards in it: ten face up and one face down on the top.

7. They should continue doing this until they have four piles. There will most probably be some piles uncapped, with a number facing upwards. You should now add together the numbers at the top of these piles and ask your audience member to count out this number of cards from the remainder of the deck, placing them face up.

ADD UP these TWO NUMBERS and THEN COUNT OUT that NUMBER of CARDS FROM the MAIN PACK

For example, if the top numbers from all the piles added together comes to sixteen, get them to count out sixteen more cards. Miraculously, the card they count to will be the card chosen at the beginning. On the very rare occasion that all the piles are capped, turn over the card that is capping the fourth pile, and this will be the chosen card!

THE _CHOSEN_ CARD!

Acknowledgements

A lot of people have helped the words I typed on my laptop become the book-shaped object in your hands, and I am extremely grateful to every one of them. So here goes...

Firstly, I would like to thank my wife, Rachel. Without your love and support none of this would be possible. Thank you for your kindness and patience – particularly when I have that glazed look when a new idea pops into my head, and the glazed look I have when one doesn't.

I'm incredibly grateful to my agent, Kirsty McLachlan at Morgan Green Creatives. Without your skills in promoting, advising, and supporting, there would be no book. I'm very fortunate indeed to have you as my agent. Thank you.

I also want to thank everyone at Walker Books. My brilliant editors, Frances Taffinder and Emily McDonnell, the guidance from Denise Johnstone-Burt, and the support and help of Rebecca Oram. I really appreciate everything you do.

A big thank you to Flavia Sorrentino for producing another stunning set of illustrations and a beautiful cover. Also, to Maia Fjord and Rebecca J Hall for so expertly putting it all together. You've made this book beautiful, just like the last one.

I'm also very grateful to LimbPower, a charity doing wonderful things to help amputees and individuals with limb difference, for their help in accurately portraying Flick. Thank you.

And lastly, a massive thank you to every teacher, TA, librarian, blogger, fellow author, and bookseller that has supported the Great Fox series. Your kindness and enthusiasm in getting books into readers' hands is overwhelming. In particular I would like to thank (deep breath) Heather at Reading Rocks, Jacqui Sydney, Karen Wallee, Chris Soul, Scott Evans (The Reader Teacher), Christopher Edge, Darren Simpson, Jamie Russell, Jennifer Killick, Thomas Taylor, M.G. Leonard, Clare Povey, Kate Heap, Alex Evelyn, Emma Suffield, Valda Varadinek, Mr Ripley, Nikki Gamble, Jennie Edspire, Tom Griffiths, Jane Etheridge, Library Girl Jo, Books for Topics, Erin Hamilton, Gavin Hetherington, and many, many others. I'm hugely grateful to you all. Thank you for all that you do to promote reading for pleasure.

JUSTYN EDWARDS graduated from the University of Southampton with a degree in archaeology. Since then he has worked as a caravan park attendant, a paperboy and a software engineer, but never as an archaeologist. He has always wanted to be a writer, and his inspiration for his debut novel, *The Great Fox Illusion*, came from watching magic shows. He realized that what elevates the tricks magicians perform are the stories they tell their audience. And in turn, stories themselves are a kind of magic trick, with authors choosing when to reveal their secrets to the reader. And so this series was born. Justyn lives in Cornwall with his wife and two cats. Visit his website at www.justynedwards.com

We hope you enjoyed

We'd love to hear from you!

#TheGreatFox
@WalkerBooksUK
@JustynEdwards